"I want Brooks

Holly's son said as s...
that yucky guy you'r...

Holly felt her face tu...
accept that her sweet little boy had been smart and
tricky enough to pull this stunt just so she would
meet the man standing in the doorway. She looked
over at Brooks—who was about to burst out
laughing.

"You're grounded—maybe for your whole life,"
she told her son, giving him a good-night kiss
before turning off the light.

Then she was back in the narrow hallway with a
tall, powerfully built man who was making no
attempt to contain his smile.

Dear Reader,

Book 1000?! In 1982, when Silhouette Special Edition was first published, that seemed a far distant goal. And now, fourteen years later, here we are!

We're opening CELEBRATION 1000 with a terrific book from the beloved Diana Palmer—*Maggie's Dad*. Diana was one of the first authors to contribute to Special Edition, and now she's returned with this tender tale of love reborn.

Lindsay McKenna continues her action-packed new series, MORGAN'S MERCENARIES: LOVE AND DANGER. The party goes on with *Logan's Bride* by Christine Flynn—the first of three tales of love and weddings. And join the festivities with wonderful stories by Jennifer Mikels, Celeste Hamilton and Brittany Young.

We have so many people to thank for helping us to reach this milestone. Silhouette Special Edition would not be what it is today without our marvellous writers. And our very special thanks to our readers. Your imaginations and brave hearts allow books to take flight—and all of us can never thank you enough for that!

The celebration continues in May and June—with books by Nora Roberts, Debbie Macomber and many more of your favourite writers! Happy Book 1000—to each and every romantic!

All the best,

The Editors

The Daddy Quest

CELESTE HAMILTON

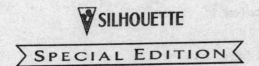

SILHOUETTE

> SPECIAL EDITION <

First published in Great Britain 1996
by Silhouette Books, Eton House, 18-24 Paradise Road,
Richmond, Surrey TW9 1SR

© Jan Hamilton Powell 1995

Silhouette, Silhouette Special Edition and Colophon are
Trade Marks of Harlequin Enterprises II B.V.

ISBN 0 373 09994 0

23-9604

Made and printed in Great Britain

For some of the special friends writing has brought into my life—
Faith Garner, Beverly Hise, Pam Monroe, Sharon Rose, Susan
Sawyer and Clara Wimberly.
Thanks for your support, guys!

CELESTE HAMILTON

has been writing since she was ten years old, with the encouragement of parents who told her she could do anything she set out to do and teachers who helped her refine her talents.

The media captured her interest in school, and she graduated from the University of Tennessee with a B.S. in communications. From there, she began writing and producing commercials at a Chattanooga, Tennessee, radio station.

Celeste began writing romances in 1985 and now works at her craft full-time. Married to a policeman, she likes nothing better than spending time at home with him and their two much-loved cats, although she and her husband also enjoy travelling when their busy schedules permit. Wherever they go, however, "It's always nice to come home to east Tennessee—one of the most beautiful corners of the world."

Other Silhouette Books by Celeste Hamilton

Silhouette Special Edition

Torn Asunder
Silent Partner
A Fine Spring Rain
Face Value
No Place to Hide
Don't Look Back
Baby, It's You
Single Father
Father Figure
Child of Dreams
Sally Jane Got Married

Which Way Is Home?
A Family Home

Silhouette Desire

*The Diamond's Sparkle
*Ruby Fire
*The Hidden Pearl

*Aunt Eugenia's
   Treasures trilogy

MY QUEST

by Zane MacPherson, age 9½
Woodmere Elementary School

I promise to search for a dad who—

1. is strong and brave

2. won't call me stupid nicknames

3. is cool about guy stuff

4. will treat Mom real nice

5. and love her, too

And I have to find him real fast before
she marries some geek.

Signed, Zane MacPherson

Zane MacPherson

Prologue

quest: a seeking or a hunt, like those under-taken by knights in the Middle Ages.

Zane MacPherson stared down at the definition instead of his math problems. Mom would be up here soon to check on him, and he would be in trouble when she saw he was only half-done. But was it his fault that thoughts of knights and ladies and battles and knightly quests were more interesting than fractions?

Sitting back in his desk chair, Zane studied the poster of a massive stone castle that had recently joined the photographs of star athletes on his room's crowded walls. He and his mom had found the poster last weekend at the mall, and he had begged to have it.

Because he was a knight, after all. A Knight of the Woodmere Realm. That's what Mr. Robinson called all the boys in the class that met on Tuesdays after school in the gym.

Zane knew what the class was really all about. He and the rest of the eleven fourth-grade knights were all boys who didn't have dads or grandfathers or step-fathers in their homes. "Boys without significant males in their lives"—that's what the registration form Mom had filled out had said. Zane had read it himself and asked his Nana Flora what *significant* meant. And at first the class had made him mad. Just because he and the other guys didn't have dads shouldn't mean they had to stay after school. But it had turned out to be fun. They got to mess around in the gym. And Mr. Robinson was cool, giving them sweatshirts that said Knights and talking to them about all kinds of junk, real man stuff. Last week Mr. Robinson had given out this definition and challenged them each to find a quest.

"You decide what your quest will be," he had said. "But make it a noble cause, an unselfish one, like any good knight would do. Search for ways to improve your grades or help at home or make people happy."

Zane had been thinking and thinking about what his own quest would be. It couldn't be something ordi-nary, like cleaning up his room or remembering to feed Wondercat. Those were all good quests, but the top quest, the big one, needed to be more important, spe-cial—

"Finished with your homework, Sir Zane?"

He turned with a guilty start to face his mother, who stood in the doorway. He grabbed his pencil. "Al-most."

"Need some help?" The masculine voice came from the man who appeared just behind his mother and slipped an arm around her shoulders. It was Joel Preston, the guy who had been hanging around a lot lately.

Struggling not to scowl because Mom said that was bad manners, Zane just shook his head.

"You've got five minutes to finish," Mom warned. "Then go say good-night to Nana and get into bed."

"Hey, Tiger," Joel said, forcing Zane to look at him. "I was telling your mom it might be fun to go to the zoo this weekend. What do you think?"

Tiger? The zoo? Who did this guy think he was talking to—some eight-year-old baby? Zane started a protest, but his mom's warning expression cut him off. Instead, he made himself smile and mumbled, "Sure." Then he turned quickly back to his homework because he was afraid if he looked at Joel a minute longer he would puke.

Zane sensed them standing in the doorway a few moments, but breathed a sigh of relief when they were gone. Zooming through the rest of his math, he kept thinking of Joel's arm around his mom. He was still thinking about it as he got ready for bed and visited his Nana Flora's room to say good-night. He was frowning by the time his mom appeared at his bedside.

She pulled the covers up to his chin and sat down on the edge of his bed. "Joel's not so bad, you know."

"He's boring."

"You don't even know him."

"I don't want to."

"Oh, Zane." Her sigh dissolved into a smile as she bent forward and kissed his forehead.

Zane pretended to squirm although he really liked this nightly kiss, liked his mother's sweet, familiar smell, liked the way she looked—all soft and pretty and young, not like so many of his friends' mothers.

He didn't know why she bothered with guys like Joel. Stiff guys, all dressed up in their white shirts and ties. Maybe he could understand her wanting to get married. He knew it wasn't always easy for her. Nana Flora said his mom worked too hard at the hospital taking care of sick people, then worked too hard at home taking care of them with no one to help her. Zane wouldn't mind his mother having some help and wouldn't mind having a dad, but not some wimpy geek like Joel, who called him stupid nicknames and wanted to visit the zoo.

"Maybe you need some help finding the right guy," Zane suggested as his mom stood.

"Are you volunteering to help me look?" Chuckling, she switched off the lamp, said a last good-night and left before Zane could reply.

He lay still, his mind racing. *This was it! His quest. He could find just the right man for Mom, the right dad for him.*

Grinning, he turned on his side and imagined a big, strong knight astride a great horse, riding toward the castle where Zane and his mother waited. It was a sure bet that knight would never call him "Tiger."

Somehow, somewhere, Zane had to find him.

Chapter One

Struggling under the weight of the injured man he carried over his shoulder, Brooks Casey rushed through the automatic-opening doors to a nearly deserted emergency room. "I need a doctor." He flashed his badge to the people behind the reception desk. "He's a police officer, and he's been shot!"

An orderly and a nurse came running. Young Dan Markowitz was lifted from Brooks's grasp to a gurney, where he groaned and rolled to his right side, exposing his wound.

"Oh, my," the lanky orderly muttered.

"What's your problem?" the nurse snapped as they hurried the gurney through swinging doors and into the treatment area. Brooks was right behind them.

"Looks like he took it in the butt."

"Oh, God," Markowitz groaned, lifting an arm over his face.

Brooks glared at the orderly, who had begun to grin. "You think a wound to the rear isn't serious, bud?"

"Oh, I know it's serious." Though the orderly tried to contain it, his smile grew even wider. "I was stationed at the hospital at Fort Benning, and we saw lots of injuries like this during the first week of firearm training. I know just how sore this dude is gonna be."

With another moan, Markowitz rolled completely over on his belly, his rump arching in the air as the gurney was swung into a curtained cubicle in the treatment room. The nurse urged him to lie down, then called for a doctor.

Still glowering, Brooks asked the orderly, "Are you implying this is a self-inflicted wound?"

"Yes, sir, I am."

"Well...you're right." And that's when Brooks lost his own struggle with the laughter he had suppressed ever since it became clear Markowitz wasn't seriously hurt. The orderly joined in. Markowitz cursed. The gray-haired, businesslike nurse shushed them all.

And, of course, she was right. Brooks guiltily tried to stop laughing, well aware a gunshot wound, however it happened, was never funny. Besides the obvious potential for a tragic injury, tonight's incident had blown an important stakeout. Brooks should be screaming about that instead of laughing over Markowitz's embarrassing situation. Yet for the love of God, Brooks couldn't imagine exactly how Markowitz managed to fire into his left cheek. The whole thing seemed unreasonably, ridiculously hilarious.

On the gurney, Markowitz was still muttering profanities. "Get out of here, Casey. I don't want you laughing over me while I bleed to death."

The nurse jerked her head at Brooks. "If you can't be an adult, then get out of here. We've got to cut this man out of his pants."

Trying his best to control a fresh burst of inappropriate laughter, Brooks backed away. Another nurse and a doctor pushed past him into the cubicle. Brooks came to rest against the wall just outside, and stood, shaking with silent guffaws.

A few moments later, the orderly was sent out, as well. He came to stand beside Brooks. They both wiped tears from their eyes and tried to stop laughing.

"How'd he do it?" the orderly finally managed to ask.

Pushing back his worn leather jacket to reveal his holster, Brooks grasped his automatic. "Near as I can tell, he was pulling out his gun and accidentally squeezed the trigger—"

"And the bullet grazed his butt," the orderly completed. Again, they dissolved into laughter.

Then Brooks looked down and into a pair of very curious, very wide, brown eyes. His laughter died, and he elbowed his companion, nodding toward their audience. The orderly's chuckles faded, as well.

"Well, it ain't really funny," the orderly muttered as he went back into the cubicle. "Ain't nothin' funny about guns."

"No, there's not." Brooks continued to gaze at the brown-eyed boy who was peering at him from around the edge of a nearby curtain.

The boy, who Brooks figured to be nine or ten, stepped out, hands thrust in the pockets of his jeans. He looked toward Markowitz's cubicle. "He shot himself?"

"It was an accident."

A series of groans emanated from Markowitz behind the curtain.

The boy asked Brooks, "Why was it funny?"

"It wasn't . . . I mean, it shouldn't have been."

"Then why were you laughing?"

Another groan led to a string of curses, and Brooks decided this wasn't the best place for this boy or this conversation. With a hand on the kid's shoulder, he guided him back into the cubicle where he had been standing. Markowitz's voice and the activities of the medical personnel were somewhat muffled by the curtains. "What are you doing back here?" Brooks asked the boy.

"I followed you."

The straightforward reply took Brooks by surprise. "Followed me? Why?"

The boy shrugged.

Brooks didn't figure the reason was all that important. "You need to get back where you belong. Were you out front?"

"I was waiting for my mom."

Brooks pushed the curtain aside again, indicating the boy should precede him out. But the youngster stopped him by asking, "Can I see your gun?"

Now more than ever, Brooks regretted acting like such a damn fool over Markowitz's injury. No one knew better than a police officer the deadly serious destruction that could be wrought by the slip of a finger on the trigger. The truth was that Markowitz was lucky the bullet only took a chunk out of his backside.

"Well, little man." Brooks pulled his gun out of his holster. "I shouldn't have laughed." He held the gun out sideways toward the boy, who gazed at the gray metal with a mixture of fascination and fear. "Guns aren't for play and they aren't for laughing about, and it isn't one bit funny when someone gets shot. The way we were laughing was just plain wrong."

The youngster seemed to have forgotten the laughter now that he faced the forbidden allure of a real gun. "Can I touch it?"

Denial rose instantly to Brooks's lips, but then he reconsidered. He thought being straight with this kid would make the best impression. And there was nothing straighter or more realistic than the feel of a gun in your hand. He remembered his own first encounter with the cold, heavy steel. He recalled how the real thing had felt less like a toy than he had expected, and he had never forgotten his father explaining, in straightforward terms, exactly what could happen if a gun were mishandled. After having acted like such an irresponsible jerk here tonight, maybe he needed to do some candid talking with this young man.

Brooks quickly emptied the ammo, crouched down beside the boy, took his hand and closed his fingers around the gun.

The kid's mouth formed a silent "Wow."

"What's your name?" Brooks asked, carefully keeping his hand around the boy's.

"Zane MacPherson."

"I'm Lieutenant Brooks Casey, Memphis P.D. Ever held a gun before, Zane?"

"My Papa Jake's. He was a policeman like you."

"He's your father?"

"He was my mom's grandfather, but he's dead now."

"I bet he told you guns were serious business, and I bet he—"

The curtains jerked back, and Brooks confronted a pair of eyes as brown as Zane's. Only these eyes were snapping with fury instead of curiosity, and they belonged to an auburn-haired woman. A very attractive woman. Brooks took in shining hair, creamy skin and curves that even her serviceable nurse's garb didn't disguise.

"What are you doing?" she demanded of Brooks.

He took the gun away while she pulled Zane to her side. "What are you doing with my son?"

"Mom—"

"What are you doing?" she repeated, voice rising.

Straightening from his crouch, Zane thrust the gun back in his holster and fished his badge out of his pocket. "I'm an officer, ma'am—"

She spared barely a glance at his shield. "So?"

"Mom, please," Zane pleaded. "We were just—"

"Let me explain to her," Brooks said. He quickly told her how he and Zane had come to be talking with one another. But the more he said, the more he felt her anger increasing. He finished with a rather lame-sounding "I just wanted to get across to your son that guns are nothing to laugh about."

"So you put a gun in his hand?"

Her scathing tone irritated Brooks, but he held on to his cool. "Ma'am, I'm sorry if you're upset, but I was just—"

"Just telling him to 'do as I say, not as I do.'"

Brooks felt angry color flood his cheeks, mostly anger at himself because she was right. "Now, listen—"

"First you laugh about a fellow officer being injured, then you urge my son to respect the destructive power of the gun." She drew Zane closer to her side. "Excuse me if I don't commend you for your efforts."

Eyes narrowed, Brooks felt some of his anger redirecting itself toward her. "I said I was wrong, ma'am. I think the boy is old enough and bright enough to appreciate that, to learn from it."

"And I think you ought to get out of here before I have you thrown out."

"Mom!" Zane protested, finally getting free of her grasp. "The gun was no big deal. Honest."

"Yes, it was," Brooks and the woman said at the same time. Then they glared at each other in silence.

Brooks spoke first, turning to Zane. "Guns are a big deal. No matter how stupid I acted here tonight, that's what I believe and that's the way I usually act. You just remember that."

"I'll make sure he does." The boy's mother tilted her chin in challenge and once more pulled him close to her side. He squirmed, but she held firm.

Cutting words sprang to Brooks's lips, but he bit them back, settling for a caustic "Yeah, right."

The woman sucked in her breath. "What do you mean by that?"

This time Brooks didn't hesitate. "Just that I have to question what a boy this age is doing wandering around a hospital emergency room by himself. That doesn't say much about your abilities to keep him safe."

Her pretty mouth tightened. "He was supposed to be waiting for me out front. I'm just coming off duty."

"But he wasn't waiting, was he? He said he followed me back here."

Zane sent a distressed look up at his mother. "I just wanted to see what had happened to the other officer. I knew to stay out of everyone's way."

"You should have stayed out front," she admonished. "You know better than to come back here."

Brooks snorted. "Even the waiting room is no place for a child. He should be at home."

That earned another glare from Zane's mother. "Thank you so much for that enlightened bit of child-rearing advice. I'm sure your own little woman is at home tending your brood with no need to earn a living or cope with the reality that sometimes a child can't be at home having milk and cookies."

That tirade sent the last of Brooks's patience up in smoke. "For your information, I have seven younger brothers and sisters, so I do know something about child rearing, even though there's no woman, little or otherwise, tending any brood of mine—"

"But since you're not a parent, especially not a *single, working parent,* you have no right to criticize someone who is."

"And you shouldn't—"

"—say anything more." The graying nurse who had been tending Markowitz stood nearby, hands on her hips, a frown creasing her smooth, coffee-colored skin. She glared first at Zane and his mother and then at Brooks. "I think y'all should break up this discussion or at the very least take it some place else."

"I'm sorry, Mrs. Coulter," Zane's mother murmured, embarrassment painting her cheeks pink.

The nurse just arched her eyebrow, then turned to Brooks, her animosity toward him clear in her sarcastic tone. "Just in case you're over being amused by what happened and want to know, your fellow officer's going to be fine. He'd like you to call his wife. That is if you're finished arguing with Nurse MacPherson."

Not bothering to answer, Brooks wheeled away to get the telephone number from Markowitz.

Behind him, he heard the nurse say, "Holly, if Zane is going to wait for you on Wednesday nights, he's going to have to stay put. I know it's not busy tonight, but you know the policy on this."

"I'm sorry," Zane chimed in. "It's my fault, Mrs. Coulter, not Mom's."

Glancing over his shoulder, Brooks caught the distress on Zane's face. Those feelings were mirrored in his mother's expression. Unlike the sharp-tongued mother tigress who had faced him only moments before, she now looked tired and vulnerable and hardly old enough to be the parent of this strapping young boy. But there was no denying Zane was her son. They had the same eyes, the same tip-tilted noses sprinkled with a dusting of freckles. The only difference was that

Zane's hair was dark brown, while hers glinted with fiery highlights.

Brooks felt his irritation with her slip away. He was ashamed of the way he had talked to her, the snap judgments he had made. Mrs. Coulter continued speaking to her in low tones, probably reading her the riot act. He looked back at Zane, who was now studying Brooks with an unfathomable expression in his wide eyes. All Brooks could think to do was send the boy a salute. He got an impish but reassuring grin in return.

Smiling, he swung into the cubicle where Markowitz was lying facedown on the gurney. Brooks resisted the urge to indulge in any "pain in the butt" jokes and instead took the time to reassure the young officer and apologize for his own breach of professional conduct.

And when Brooks emerged moments later with Markowitz's home phone number, he was disappointed that Zane and his mother were nowhere to be seen.

He called his partner's wife and his department superior, then stopped Mrs. Coulter near the reception desk. "Is Mrs. MacPherson gone?"

"Why?"

"Because I wanted to apologize to her."

The nurse scrutinized him with a sharp, all-seeing gaze. Brooks was suddenly aware of how he must look in his ragged jeans, old jacket and with three days' growth of dark beard on his chin.

"We were on a stakeout," he explained, combing a hand through his hair. "We needed to look the part."

Making no comment on that, Mrs. Coulter began flipping through the medical chart she held. "Miss MacPherson and her son are gone."

"*Miss* MacPherson?"

"That's what I said. She's gone."

"Then I'll call her tomorrow if she'll be working."

Closing the chart with an emphatic snap, she looked up at him in irritation. "You can call, yes, but don't get your hopes up about her being interested in the likes of you."

Blinking in surprise, Brooks took a step backward. "What does that mean?"

"Nothing. But if Holly MacPherson weighed two-fifty and had a mustache, you wouldn't be so all-fired concerned about calling and apologizing, now would you?"

The woman marched off down the hall before Brooks could sputter a protest. From behind the reception desk, the orderly he had been laughing with earlier regarded him with a sympathetic roll of his eyes. Brooks started to say something, then just closed his mouth and went outside into the cool, early November night air to wait for Markowitz's wife.

He silently berated himself for his actions this evening. He had behaved with disrespect in regard to a fellow officer's injury, a disrespect he had communicated to the E.R. staff and to a young, impressionable boy. Then he had been argumentative and judgmental with the boy's mother.

The boy's very pretty mother.

Brooks laid his head back on the rough concrete wall. He had to admit Mrs. Coulter could be right. If Zane MacPherson's mother weren't a knockout, would he be so intent on apologizing? Maybe not. And Lord, his own mama would be ashamed of him for that.

Yet he believed even his mother would forgive a few of the thoughts he was having about the sweet face and luscious curves of *Miss* MacPherson. In fact, mama just might be relieved if she knew about those thoughts, considering how much she worried about his bachelor status.

"Maybe I'll tell her," Brooks murmured. Then he grinned at the improbable image of his sharing a sexual fantasy with his straitlaced mama. She might have borne eight children, and he might be an adult aged thirty-three, but sex still wasn't something he would be discussing with her anytime soon.

Sex wasn't a subject he should even be thinking about since there was no woman in his life right now. There'd been no one since his last relationship had ended last summer over his inability to get serious. Of course, he had told the woman in question from the beginning that he wasn't interested in being serious, but that didn't seem to matter to most women. Even the ones who started out saying they wanted to keep it light ended up wanting a commitment.

Right now, he had other matters to think about. Like what his superiors would say if Markowitz reported how he had acted tonight. And like what he and the young officer were both going to say about blowing their surveillance of a drug ring, a surveillance that had taken them weeks to put in place.

A car jerked to a stop at the curb, and Brooks's boss got out. Tall and hefty without being fat, Captain Dixon was a bigger man than Brooks, who, at six-three and nearly two hundred pounds, was no lightweight. And tonight, with a thunderous scowl on his face, Dixon seemed even bigger and tougher than ever. Brooks braced himself for an onslaught.

Dixon waited until he was practically in Brooks's face before growling, "Just what in the hell have you done this time?"

"But Zane couldn't have just gone off without telling someone." Holly MacPherson's protest was greeted with silence from the two other women in the room.

Flora MacPherson, called Nana Flora by all who loved her, pushed away from the kitchen table with a disgusted snort. "Well, he isn't here, and we don't know where he is, do we?"

"He said he'd be at Marcus's," Holly stated, as she'd been doing ever since Nana Flora had called her at work to report that Zane and Marcus were missing.

Marcus's mother, Charleen, their next-door neighbor, folded her arms across her midriff. "Marcus said that he would be over here, that he and Zane were working on a project together. I figured Nana Flora would be watching the boys, so I took a little extra time at school myself, making lesson plans for next week."

The older woman shook her head. "I'm making costumes for a production over at the community theater. I wasn't worried, because Zane said he'd be at your house. I wasn't home until five. That's when I came over to fetch Zane."

"And when I found out those two rascals put one over on us again..." Charleen bit her lip. "Where in the world are those boys?"

"God only knows," Nana Flora intoned in her usual dramatic way.

Holly squeezed her grandmother's arm in reassurance. "Let's not panic." But the horrible things that could happen to two nine-year-old boys on their own began flashing through her head as she glanced out at the deserted backyard. Raindrops drizzled down the kitchen window, blurring her view. It was now after six, already growing dark on this cool and wet November evening.

"I'm calling the police," Nana Flora announced.

"Let's make sure we've called all their friends first," Holly cautioned.

Charleen nodded. "I've already called Marcus's dad. I'll send Bob out in the neighborhood as soon as he gets home. Let's split up the list of people to call, and I'll do some of the phoning from my house."

They made their lists quickly, and Charleen left while Nana Flora wrung her hands and paced the floor. When Holly had phoned the last name with no luck and Charleen called to report the same, the older woman let out a cry of despair.

"Now, just stop it," Holly told her, more sharply than she would talk to her grandmother under other circumstances. "Bob's out combing the street with one of the other fathers from the neighborhood. We need to just sit tight until they report in." As Nana wrung her hands, Holly fought to hold on to her patience. Much as she loved this woman, much as she owed her, there were times when Flora's melodramatics wore on Holly's nerves.

"Zane's just a baby," Nana Flora murmured.

"He's nine and half years old and he knows better than to take off like this."

"But what if somebody—"

"Don't say it," Holly interrupted her, taking hold of the woman's hands. "Don't say anyone took him, don't even think it. This is just another of his and Marcus's little adventures."

Nodding silently, Nana Flora squared her shoulders, drawing herself up to her full five-foot height. For all her excitability, she was a strong woman, and she had always been there for Holly.

Flora and Papa Jake had raised Holly since she was three, when their son died and Holly's mother had decided she wasn't up to raising a child on her own. They had been good to her, patient, kind and gentle. Because of them, she had never felt the lack of parents. And when Holly was eighteen, pregnant, unmarried, and deserted by Zane's immature father, they had accepted her decision to keep her baby. She had known they were disappointed in her, but they had stood by her just the same. Their unconditional support and financial sacrifices had propelled her through college and into a career in nursing. Because they taught her how to be strong, Holly had felt capable of accomplishing her goals and being a good mother to Zane. The warmth of their family love had seen them through the dark days three years ago when Papa Jake fell ill and died. Having survived that, Holly felt sure that together they could take on anything.

Nana Flora paced to the window and stared out. "I should have been home. I should have told the theater to find someone else to make these costumes."

"And turn down getting paid for something you love?" Holly crossed the room to her grandmother's side and slipped an arm around her shoulders.

Nana Flora had always worked as a seamstress to supplement Papa Jake's income. He'd been a beat cop until his retirement, his pay had never been great; the money she earned had been welcomed. Though Nana Flora had sewn for many people, it was her work with the local theater that had always brought her the most satisfaction, appealing as it did to her sense of drama. The additional income also provided some extra security. Holly made a good salary and Nana Flora drew a pension, but the expenses from Papa Jake's illness, the hefty second mortgage he had taken out on the house to pay for Holly's college and the demands of everyday life sometimes made finances tight.

"It isn't your fault that Zane has taken off like this," Holly assured her grandmother again. "Something's gotten into him lately."

She thought about earlier this week and the way Zane had followed those police officers into the emergency-room treatment area. Zane's deliberate disobedience was uncharacteristic. The big, rough-looking cop who had been showing Zane his gun had said the emergency room was no place for a child. And no matter how angry his know-it-all macho manner had made Holly, she figured he was probably right. But on the other hand, what was she supposed to do? Zane had only been at the hospital for an hour. Nana Flora had dropped him off at six on the way to her bridge club, the only recreation the woman allowed herself two nights a month. Holly was working a seven-to-seven shift, none of his usual sitters was available, and she was sure Zane was old enough to stay put for an hour. He had done it before. And just because he had disobeyed her didn't mean she was a bad, neglectful mother, despite what that cop had implied.

But what would that cop say now, when her son was missing? When there had been no one here to see that Zane got home from school? When she had just assumed he would be safe and sound at their neighbor's house?

Holly had little difficulty imagining what that cop would say. She had no trouble visualizing his disapproving expression. Those scathing blue eyes and the scornful twist of his irregular but oddly handsome features.

Closing her eyes, she erased his image. She was never likely to see him again, and what he or anyone else thought of her was of no concern right now. All that mattered was that Zane and Marcus showed up safe and sound, the sooner the better.

"Zane doesn't like Joel," Nana Flora said, breaking into Holly's thoughts.

She blinked, momentarily confused. "Joel?"

"Remember? That prissy guy you've been dating."

"Joel isn't prissy."

Nana Flora sniffed. "He's as dull as dog food."

"Nana!"

"I can't help it." She threw up her hands. "I have to tell the truth. He's dull and boring, and Zane can't stand him. So if you're wondering what's gotten into your son, you might think about the man you're choosing to keep company with."

"Joel's a nice, steady and secure man. An accountant."

"He counts beans."

Holly frowned. "He manages the financial affairs of several successful companies. He's very settled and responsible, and I happen to think he'd make a wonderful father."

"Hah!" Going to the refrigerator, Nana Flora began pulling out leftovers. "Sometimes I don't understand you, Holly. It takes more than money or security to make a man good father material."

"But money doesn't hurt," Holly replied, turning back to peer anxiously out the window. "And neither does security. In case you've forgotten, I got involved with someone poor but exciting once before. You see what that got me."

There was a moment of silence before Nana Flora murmured, "It brought us Zane, so I don't count it all bad."

Zane. Holly leaned her forehead against the window's cool glass. Her brown-eyed boy, the child she had loved so fiercely from the moment she knew he rested in her womb. The mischievous scamp who was out in the rain right now, alone. Zane's pet, Wondercat, wound himself around Holly's legs and meowed. The mournful sound underscored Holly's foreboding, and she shivered. Instantly, Nana Flora was at Holly's side, soothing her.

Across the room, the door to the side porch flew open, admitting a shower of rain along with Charleen, Bob, Marcus, Zane and...*Zane!* Holly was so happy to see her son that she hurried to his side without pausing to check out the other person who accompanied him.

She dropped to her knees in the puddle of water Zane's sneakers made on the linoleum, pulled him into her arms and held him for a long moment. Then she drew back and gave him a little shake. "Where have you been?"

"With me."

She glanced up and took in blue eyes and strong, masculine features framed by unruly, damp black hair. Holly sank back on her heels. "You."

The cop she figured she'd never see again put out a big hand. Without thinking, Holly slipped her fingers into his and let him help her to her feet. "You," she said again, unnecessarily.

"Lieutenant Brooks Casey." A faint grin teased the corners of his mouth. "And from the look on your face, I must be your worst nightmare."

Chapter Two

Part one of the quest—complete.

Grinning in triumph, Zane tugged on the sweat-pants and T-shirt he wore as pajamas. He knew he was in trouble over what had happened today, but he'd done what he'd intended. Right now, Brooks Casey was sitting down in the kitchen, talking to his mom and Nana Flora. Even if his mom didn't see what a cool guy and excellent father-type person Brooks was, his grandmother would. And as Zane had known for as long as he could remember, when Mom needed convincing, having Nana Flora on his side was a big help. After tonight, he'd have an ally if he needed one.

Trying hard to contain a squeal of excitement, Zane leapt into the center of his bed at about the same moment a knock sounded on his door.

He was scrambling into a sitting position when his mother came in, carrying a tray of food. "Zane Jacob MacPherson, haven't I told you not to jump on your bed?"

As usual, her uncanny ability to see what he was doing, even through a closed door, amazed Zane. "I'm sorry," he mumbled, sitting back against the pillows arranged at the headboard. Wondercat settled at his side.

His mom set the tray on the table beside his bed. "I hope you hung your wet clothes over the bathtub like I asked."

"Yes, ma'am."

"And I hope you're not ever going to do something like this again."

"It was no big deal, Mom."

"Going all across town and getting this cop—"

"Brooks," Zane put in. "His name is Brooks. He was named for the third baseman Brooks Robinson, who played for the Baltimore Orioles a bunch of years ago. He was like the best third baseman there ever was. Brooks's father is from Baltimore and he loves baseball and so he named—"

"Drink this milk." Cutting him off, his mom handed him a glass, then settled the tray over his knees, shooed away the cat and sat down on the edge of the bed. "Eat this sandwich and chips. Then I want you asleep."

"But it's Friday, Mom. And it's barely past seven o'clock."

"After what you did today, you're lucky I'm just sending you to bed. You're grounded for two weeks from everything except your Knights club."

"Aw, Mom," Zane grumbled around a mouthful of sandwich, although the punishment was about what he had expected.

"No arguments. Because of you and Marcus, I had to come home early from work, and you had all of us terrified. You can't go around thinking you can run off like that." She brushed his hair off his forehead, something Zane usually tried to dodge. But he had seen how upset she was, so he figured some babying was the least he could submit to. He knew it made her feel better.

"It wasn't Marcus's fault," he said after draining the glass of milk and polishing off most of the food. "It was my idea."

"But why did you want to ride the bus across town all alone?"

They had already gone over this down in the kitchen before Marcus and his parents went home. Zane would just as soon not have to tell the story again. "Just because."

"That's not a good enough reason."

Zane avoided looking right at her. It was tough to lie, even when he knew it was for a good cause. "It just seemed like fun."

"But when you didn't have enough money to ride back to our neighborhood, you knew to go to the police station."

"Uh-huh."

"And to ask for Mr. Casey."

"*Lieutenant* Casey. I remembered meeting him the other night."

His mother plucked some of the chips from his plate and crunched them for a moment. When Zane looked

up, she was watching him with what he thought of as
her X-ray eyes, the ones she used when she wanted to
see what was in his head. "Why didn't you just call me
or Nana or Charleen or Bob?"

"I was hoping I could get home without you knowing where I'd been, 'cause I knew you'd be mad. And
besides, when Brooks told us he *had* to call you, both
your lines were busy, so he just brought us home."

She ate another chip. "I don't think you're telling
me everything, Zane."

From the doorway, Brooks said, "Don't you think
you ought to 'fess up to your mom?"

Zane watched his mom frown as the big policeman
came to the foot of his bed. Brooks seemed to fill up
half the room, not much like that wimp-o-rama, Joel.

"Mr. Casey," his mom said, getting up from the
bed.

"Just 'Brooks,' okay?" He smiled at her, but Zane
saw that she didn't respond. And he knew that wasn't
good.

"He took real good care of me and Marcus," Zane
said, trying to help matters along between them.

"I'm sure he did," his mother murmured.

Brooks regarded Zane sternly. "I think it's about
time you told me and your mom exactly what you were
up to tonight. That's why I asked your grandmother
if I could come on up here, so I could hear the truth."

Zane opened his mouth, ready to offer the same
explanation he had already given, but his mom interrupted. "Mr. Casey, if you don't mind, *I'll* find out
what Zane was up to. I do appreciate you taking care
of him, and I can assure you this won't ever happen

again." She walked to the door. "I know you probably have somewhere you need to be."

"Not really—"

"But we don't want to hold you up any longer," she said in the sort of tone Zane had learned not to cross.

It was a tone Brooks seemed to know, as well, because he just shrugged. "All right, Miss MacPherson. I'll be going." He saluted Zane just as he'd done the other night at the hospital, just the way Papa Jake used to. "See you around, little man." The nickname was also the same one his grandfather had used, the only nickname Zane could stand, a much better nickname than "Tiger."

"I'll see you out," his mom told Brooks.

Brooks was going to leave. Walk out too soon. I can't let it happen, Zane thought. *I can't. Not after everything me and Marcus went through to get him here. From the minute I saw Brooks carry his friend into the hospital, I knew he was the one. The right one. For me and Mom.*

"Wait," he called out.

Both Brooks and his mom turned to face him as Zane's mind raced for a ploy to keep them here together. He figured he had only one option left—the truth.

"Well?" His mother had folded her arms across her middle, a sure sign she was getting really steamed.

"I tricked you," Zane said, and the words picked up speed as the real story spilled out. "Me and Marcus rode the bus downtown and went straight to the police station. That's where we planned to go all along, to find Brooks. And we had enough money to get home in case Brooks wasn't there. But when he was, we pretended we didn't and now..." His voice trailed away as he watched his mom's face grow pale. "And now I'm sorry," he finished weakly.

No one said anything for what seemed to Zane like a long, long time.

Then Brooks spoke up, his forehead creasing in a frown. "So you came to find me on purpose. Why? Are you in some sort of trouble?"

Zane bit his lip, focusing on his mom's face. The truth didn't seem like such a good idea now, not with the way her cheeks were turning all red. But he had gone too far to turn back now. "I'm not in trouble. I just wanted you guys to...see each other."

His mom's forehead wrinkled. "See each other?"

"So you'd go out...or something. I like Brooks a whole lot better than Joel. Joel's just a dumb old guy."

Holly felt heat spread from her face down her neck. It wasn't easy to take in the knowledge that her sweet little boy had been smart enough and tricky enough to pull this stunt just so she would perhaps go out with the man standing beside her. She felt kind of dizzy. However, she was cognizant enough of her surroundings to realize the man in question was going to burst out laughing at any moment.

"Don't you dare," she muttered between clenched teeth.

He somehow managed to control himself and even sounded stern when he said to Zane, "Scaring your mother like that wasn't very smart."

Zane looked down at his tray, his mouth drooping at the corners. "I know."

"Don't do it again," Brooks added.

His jaw squaring in a way she knew all too well, Zane glared up at them. "But Joel's the geekiest guy in the whole world. I don't want him for my father."

That outburst sent Holly into action. In one quick swoop, she collected the empty milk glass and the tray and told Zane, "You are grounded for maybe your whole life. And we will discuss this tomorrow. Right now, I'm turning out the lights, and you can just lay here in bed and think about how badly you've let me down."

Less than a minute went by before Zane's lights were out and his door was shut, and she was standing in the narrow hall with a tall, powerfully built man who was now making no attempt to contain his smile.

"This is not funny," she whispered.

"You've got to give the little man some points for effort."

"Points are not what I'm thinking of giving him right now, Mr. Casey."

"For the last time, would you please call me Brooks?" Without asking, he took the tray and easily balanced it in one hand, his other hand taking hold of her elbow as they headed for the staircase.

She ignored his renewed instruction about his name and started down the stairs. "I just can't imagine what's gotten into Zane."

"Seems to me he told you. He thinks Joel is geeky."

"He doesn't really."

On the stair landing, Brooks paused and rubbed his chin thoughtfully. "So Joel isn't geeky?"

"I've been seeing Joel for several months. He's always been very nice to Zane. If he hadn't been, then I certainly wouldn't still be seeing him."

"So the two of you are pretty serious?"

"I don't know if 'serious' is the right—"

"But you love him."

"Love hasn't entered—"

"Then it's lust, basically."

That brought her up short. "What?"

"You and this Joel . . . you're involved, but not really in love and not sure it's serious, so I figure it's just some physical thing, right?"

Incensed by his presumptuous question, Holly took the tray out of his grasp and marched the rest of the way downstairs. In the foyer, she nodded toward the front door. "I'm sure you have to be going, don't you?"

He seemed not to notice the ice in her voice. "What I'm saying is that what happened today proves Zane is pretty upset about the prospect of Joel becoming his father. I don't know if it's worth upsetting him if Joel's not really going to be around too long."

Holly stared at him, stupefied. "Who said he wouldn't be around?"

"But if you don't love him—"

"I didn't say that."

Brooks looked confused. "On the stairs, you said it was lust."

"No, that's what *you* said. All I said was that Joel and I aren't all that serious."

"But you're sleeping with him."

"No, I'm not," she sputtered, though she was immediately furious with herself for giving this crass man information that was none of his business.

"You're not sleeping with him?" A slow, lopsided and totally charming smile appeared on Brooks's lips.

He stepped closer, putting his hands on either side of the tray that separated them. "Really?"

Holly was too shocked by his manner to do much more than stare at him.

His voice lowered. "If that's so, I guess Zane's right. This Joel really is just a dumb old guy."

She rocked back on her heels, all too aware that for a moment she had swayed toward him, drawn in by his deep blue eyes and the intimate tone of his voice. "What a disgusting attitude," she muttered, shoving the tray into his stomach. He caught the empty glass before it crashed to the floor, then stumbled backward.

She faced him with hands on her hips. "How completely, totally macho. Yours is just the sort of attitude that I *don't* want my son to grow up with."

"I was just being honest about what I thought."

"Insinuating that two people who are seeing one another *must* be sleeping together, isn't honesty—it's an outdated, ridiculous notion perpetuated by men like you whose thoughts emanate from their crotches, not their brains."

He seemed taken aback by her tirade. "You missed my point."

"I think not."

"All that I meant was that anyone who could date a beautiful woman like you for months without making love to her must be pretty dumb."

"So you were trying to *compliment* me?"

"Yes."

She realized then that this man, in his crude and insulting way, was attempting to convey his interest in her. Only she was definitely not interested in him.

"Mr. Casey," she said as stiffly as she could, "the fact that you think that's a compliment only proves what a Neanderthal you are."

Instead of looking angry or hurt or even discouraged, he merely nodded. "I guess this Joel isn't a Neanderthal."

"Joel is a kind and sensitive man whom I happen to really care for."

"Then why aren't you…I mean…you know." With that infuriating smile threatening to appear again, he cocked an eyebrow suggestively.

Holly was overwhelmed by the urge to smack him, a feeling completely foreign to her nature. She fought it off, but couldn't seem to formulate a comeback.

And his smile spread, completely transforming his features once more. "I've got a feeling this Joel's problems go a lot deeper than just being dumb and geeky."

Without dignifying his statement with a reply, Holly strode to the front door. She grasped the knob while she glared at Brooks over her shoulder. "I really don't know why I've let this conversation go on, other than I'm exhausted and your police training must make you very good at getting people to talk. But our conversation is over now. Thank you for bringing Zane and Marcus home. And now—" she opened the door and made a sweeping gesture to the outside "—now…you can go."

But Brooks Casey just stood in the middle of the foyer grinning like a big, self-satisfied tomcat. Behind Holly, someone cleared his throat. Turning, she found Joel standing on the porch. Nice, steady Joel— in his pressed jeans and conservative sweater, his medium blond hair neatly styled. Joel—so civilized and sophisticated and different from Brooks Casey in his rumpled shirt and old leather jacket and too-long hair.

Joel's smile was tentative as he glanced from Holly to Brooks and back again. "Something tells me you've forgotten we were going out tonight."

"Going out?"

"The movies?"

"Oh...oh, that's right. I did forget." She stood looking at Joel blankly until he cleared his throat.

"Can I come in?"

"Oh...oh, my, yes." She shook her head, trying to recover her poise. "Joel, come in and..." She shot another irritated glance toward Brooks.

Brooks stepped forward and stuck out his hand, properly introducing himself and in the process managing to dwarf Joel. Not just with his size but by virtue of the rough-edged vitality he exuded.

Joel frowned in concern as he gripped Brooks's hand. "Has there been a problem here, Officer?"

"Oh, no..." Holly began.

"Well, yes..." Brooks said at the same time.

She glared at him.

His return gaze was deliberately bland.

And she again wanted to smack him.

Instead, she began a halting explanation. Only how did she explain that Zane had caused this whole mess because he professed to dislike Joel so completely? That it was this big stranger whom Zane had picked out for her to date? Somehow, the words she needed to adequately explain the ridiculous situation just wouldn't come.

Thankfully, Holly was saved from the details by Zane and Nana Flora. Her son appeared halfway down the stairs, looking contrite and asking to talk to her. Nana Flora came out of the kitchen with the news that she had reheated last night's beef stew and made a pan of corn bread, and there was plenty for both men to have a bite to eat.

Holly would have preferred to see Brooks Casey leaving her house, but the last thing she wanted was a scene. So she entrusted both men to Nana Flora's capable hands. She took her time settling Zane in bed, listening to his genuinely contrite apology, and changing out of her uniform, hoping Brooks would be gone when she returned downstairs.

To her dismay, however, he was seated at the kitchen table, regaling Joel and Nana Flora with some tale that had them in stitches.

Brooks got up and pulled out a chair when he spied Holly standing in the doorway. "Come on in."

"Yes," Joel said, belatedly rising, as well. "Come right in, dear."

Nana Flora went to the stove and ladled a bowl of stew. "Brooks was just telling us this hilarious story about his brothers."

"Brothers?" Holly murmured with polite uninterest.

"They're twins," Brooks explained. "Several years younger than me. They were always into something."

Chuckling, Nana Flora set the steaming bowl in front of Holly. "Just imagine if we had two of Zane. What a handful."

"To say the least." Studiously avoiding the gaze of the black-haired man who had made himself so at home with her grandmother and her date, Holly accepted the stew with a smile. But inside, she was fuming. Why didn't he just leave?

Nana Flora took her chair again. "Brooks's brothers stole the family car when they were only twelve. That makes what Zane did today seem pretty tame."

"But it wasn't tame."

Joel crumbled another piece of corn bread into his stew. "I guess you're punishing him?"

"He's grounded."

"Brooks here seems to think I'm the problem," Joel continued.

Pausing with a spoonful of stew between the bowl and her mouth, Holly stared at Brooks, who gave his meal more attention than it could possibly need.

Joel kept on as if it was the most natural thing in the world for this stranger to offer him advice on Holly's son. "Brooks seems to feel that Zane might resent our relationship and that today he was just acting out and trying to get your attention. Now, Holly, you know the last thing I'd ever want to do is cause a problem with your son. And I'm not dumb. I do know that Zane hasn't exactly warmed to me—"

Nana Flora was seized by such a fit of coughing that Brooks jumped up to refill her empty water glass. Holly, who could see the amusement dancing in the depths of her grandmother's eyes, glared her disapproval, even though she was glad Joel had been interrupted. Her real aggravation was with Brooks for poking his nose in where it didn't belong.

Before she could tell him, however, he said, "If y'all will excuse me, I should be on my way."

Not bothering with any false niceties, Holly got to her feet. "I'll show you out." Though he looked amused, he didn't say anything as she led the way to the front door.

They were trailed by Nana Flora and Joel, both of whom acted as if Brooks were a good friend departing after a pleasant visit. Holly could say one thing for the man—he worked fast with his charm.

But just so he wouldn't think he was too welcome here, Holly said, "Please don't concern yourself any more about Zane. He knows this sort of thing won't be tolerated again."

Casting a quick look in Joel's direction, Brooks murmured, "Oh, I'm not worried about Zane. In fact, I think he's a pretty sharp little boy."

Holly let him go without another word, not even a goodbye, because what she really wanted to say to him was completely beyond the bounds of what she considered acceptable language. Flanked by Nana Flora and Joel, she stood on the porch and watched Brooks climb into a nondescript late-model sedan.

"Nice guy," Joel commented. "It says something good about our police department when they take time out to interest themselves in a little boy's welfare."

Another fit of coughing overtook Nana Flora. Holly didn't need to see her grandmother's face to know the woman was again fighting laughter. No doubt Nana Flora knew exactly what Zane had been up to tonight. Certainly, she had picked up on the fact that Brooks might be interested in Holly. And from the way Nana Flora had been catering to the big lug of a cop, she probably would agree with Zane that

Brooks was a highly qualified candidate for the job of Holly's husband and Zane's father.

Realizing all that, Holly responded a little more warmly than usual when Joel put his arm around her shoulders. She cuddled closer to his side, slipping her arms around his waist and laying her head on his shoulder just as the beams from Brooks's departing car swept the porch with light. Joel, innocent that he was, waved goodbye. Mumbling something under her breath, Nana Flora went inside.

And perhaps it was her imagination, but Holly thought Brooks's car shot just a little too quickly away from the curb. At any rate, brakes squealed somewhere down near the corner. She couldn't swear those brakes were Brooks's, because by that time she was busy easing out of Joel's much too amorous embrace. It was strange how kisses she had once found pleasant but unexciting had suddenly become downright distasteful.

"Hey, Mike, you ever dated a nurse?"

The portly officer seated at the desk across from Brooks didn't even look up from his paperwork. "You know I got married when I was eighteen. I never dated anyone but my wife."

"Well, I met this nurse...."

"Oh, yeah?" Interest suddenly piqued, Mike DeWitt wiggled his eyebrows suggestively. "Is it true what they say about nurses?"

Brooks laughed, falling into the familiar pattern of Monday-morning squad-room talk. "That's what I was asking you, Mike. So far, I haven't even asked this nurse out."

From the desk that faced Mike's, Detective Donna Fortnoy broke into their conversation. "You guys are pigs, you know. I don't know how these ridiculous clichés get started about women."

Mike grinned, winking at Brooks. "I always heard that clichés arise from the truth."

"Well, you heard wrong. And you guys better watch out. I'm going to have to send around another memo about politically correct on-the-job conversations." Donna's smile belied her serious tone.

Brooks laughed easily, enjoying the banter between Donna and Mike, who were partners. As part of a special narcotics task force, the three of them had worked in tandem for years and were good friends. He and Mike sometimes needled Donna about women, and she returned the favor by grousing about men. Running beneath the wisecracks, however, was a deep vein of mutual respect. Brooks had put his life in both of these cops' hands before, and he had taken theirs in his. They had shared failures, personal and professional, as well as successes. Markowitz had come on board as Brooks's partner only in the past six months, after Brooks's superiors decided he had been a lone wolf long enough. Brooks was having a few problems adjusting to having someone in his face all the time.

"How's the kid?" Mike asked Brooks, referring to Markowitz.

"He'll be back tomorrow, I guess."

Regarding him with shrewd dark eyes, Donna asked, "Did you meet the nurse when you took Markowitz into the hospital the other night?"

"Yeah." Brooks picked up the paperwork he had been struggling with before he asked Mike for his opinion on nurses. He wasn't really sure why he had brought Holly up in the first place, other than the fact that she and her son had occupied an inordinate amount of his thoughts all weekend. He kept remembering her bright, pretty face, kept thinking about the boy's ingenuity in getting Brooks over to their place. But most of all, he kept seeing Holly trapped in the high beams of his car lights as she laid her head on that loser Joel's shoulder. A loser she didn't even want to sleep with, for crying out loud. He hadn't intended to make such a big deal about that on Friday night. It had just taken him so by surprise. To Brooks's way of thinking, when two adults dated for that length of time, some things should just come naturally. How could they not come naturally with someone as alive as Holly MacPherson? Someone that attractive, that warm...

"Brooks?"

He looked up, only to find Mike and Donna watching him with interest. She said, "Are you going to tell us about this nurse or just sit there mooning about her?"

"I wasn't mooning. I was thinking."

Mike shrugged. "Mooning. Thinking. It's all semantics. And no matter which it is, I must do my duty. As I was instructed last summer when your last romantic entanglement unwound, I must remind you of your pledge not to get involved with anyone who's looking for the big *C*."

"Commitment?" Donna murmured.

"Commitment, marriage—what have you." Mike shook his head. "As we all know, our boy Brooks has made a vow of matrimonial avoidance."

"And a wise vow that might be." Sadness shadowed the dark-haired woman's expression. Her second marriage had ended in divorce just last year. "Cops and relationships don't always mix too well, as we all know."

"Yes, we do," Mike agreed glumly. Married for twenty-some years, he and his wife were in counseling right now. Both of them were having trouble dealing with the tension and demanding workload engendered by his job. "So, Brooks, be warned. Perhaps you should steer clear of the nurse."

Brooks shook his head. "You guys are something else. All I said was that I met her. You two already have me halfway down the aisle with her."

"She must have made quite an impression for you to even mention her." Donna's chair creaked as she sat back, grinning. "Come on, Casey, give us the dirt."

Wishing he had never brought this subject up, Brooks explained, "You remember the kids who showed up to see me on Friday?"

Mike tsk-tsked. "She's got kids?"

"One kid. The dark-haired boy who did all the talking on Friday."

"Oh, man," Donna murmured. "A woman with a cute kid like that. I'd say she's prime commitment material. Remember, it was the kids that first got me and my ex together. We were both looking for someone to share the responsibilities. Only now that it's over, I'm bringing up his kid, my kid and the one we had together."

Brooks sucked in a deep breath and let it out. "Yeah, you're right, Donna. This nurse and her son aren't for me."

Of course, he had known that before he ever said a word to his co-workers. Holly MacPherson hadn't liked him one bit when they met at the hospital. She liked him even less now. He was a Neanderthal, someone quite different from that skinny accountant she was dating. A skinny accountant who drove a Lexus and whose watch probably cost as much as Brooks brought home in six months.

Holly was definitely the commitment type, as well. While she had been upstairs putting Zane to bed, Brooks had taken the opportunity to do some gentle probing with Nana Flora. Holly had never married Zane's father, a coward who'd skipped out when she got pregnant. Since then, she had been dedicated to her son, her work and to her grandparents. The grandfather had been gone a few years.

"Either of you ever know a cop named Jake MacPherson?" Brooks asked his friends.

"I worked with him when I was a rookie," Mike said. "Salt-of-the-earth kind of guy."

"This nurse is Jake MacPherson's granddaughter."

"Then she's probably straight-arrow. At the very least, she might have some idea of what being a cop is all about." Mike's laughter was dry. "That's certainly more than most people know. Brooks, I bet the women you've dated in the past thought being a cop was like they show it on television. All flash and dash."

Donna stood, her arms full of file folders. "Yeah, look at all this flashy paperwork. My ex was so jealous of what he liked to call my *glamorous* job. All he ever heard me tell him were the parts where we made a bust or caught the bad guy. He never listened when I talked about the ninety-five percent of this job that's dull, repetitive frustration.''

''My wife says...''

As Mike began a story about how his wife didn't understand his work, Brooks tuned him out. Oh, he cared. He truly wanted Mike and his wife to get it together. He loved them both, liked their two kids, just as he liked Donna's three rug rats. But sometimes it seemed to Brooks he didn't know a single cop who had a decent marriage or a relationship that had worked longer than a year or two. The way he saw it, people who chose this line of work were simply asking for trouble when they got involved with someone or, God forbid, had a child.

People—his mother especially—were always telling him he was missing something by not marrying and having children. But Brooks figured he had helped raise one family—his two younger brothers and five younger sisters. Several of them were married now and had kids of their own. Brooks didn't envy them. After growing up surrounded by people, he liked having his own space, doing his own thing. That's why he had worked for years without a partner.

And that's why he was putting Holly MacPherson and her cozy little house and her sweet grandmother and her feisty little boy out of his head. He didn't need those sorts of entanglements. He was free to spend every day, all day, on his work. Free to fill every long, lonely hour with work.

Long and lonely? Brooks frowned at his choice of words. Since when were his hours long and lonely, anyway?

"My, my, my, it sure looks like the troops are busy."

As the voice broke into Brooks's reverie, he looked up at Captain Dixon, who stood in the doorway to his glassed cubicle office, surveying the squad room.

Brooks tapped his stack of unfinished reports. "We all got paperwork, Chief."

The big black man strolled down the narrow corridor between the officers' desks. He stopped beside Markowitz's empty space. "Casey, I understand why detectives DeWitt and Fortnoy have paperwork. They've actually collared a few bad guys in recent weeks. All you and Markowitz have done, on the other hand, is keep the hospital busy."

Brooks kicked back in his chair and looked up at his boss. "Maybe I just work best by myself."

"Haven't you played that tune enough to know it's not going to make me dance?"

"But, sir—"

"But nothing. You've got a partner. Learn to live with it."

Behind Dixon's back, Donna held up a drawing of the captain spitting fire. Brooks suppressed a smile and murmured a quick "Yes, sir."

"Fine." Dixon planted himself on the edge of Markowitz's desk. "I've got some news. Our friend Dante Wilson may be back in business."

His interest caught by the name, Brooks laid down his pen. "Who says?"

"One of his boys was caught making a deal on Friday night. He was pretty shook up and did a lot of talking. Then one of our undercovers spotted Dante in his old hangout Saturday night."

"The Split Nickel Bar?"

"That's it."

Mike said, "I thought Dante was in the Bahamas, mourning his loss."

Dixon shrugged. "Maybe two years in the sun is all he needed to get over the death of his son."

"Lewis Wilson," Donna murmured, catching Brooks's eye. "The old man's son. Heir to a narcotics empire."

"Until I killed him," Brooks put in, giving voice to what they were all thinking. Silence greeted his blunt statement. He kept his expression stony, trying not to reveal the turmoil inside him. Until that day over two years ago when Lewis Wilson was caught in the cross fire of a bust, Brooks had said it would be easy to kill someone like Lewis. But it hadn't been easy. It still wasn't easy to live with the knowledge that he had taken a life, even the life of no-good scum.

"You took him out before he could do the same to you." Dixon put emphasis the last word by jabbing a finger in the air. "I had hoped old Dante would just lay in the sun and count his ill-gotten gains for the rest of his life. We all know he put his worthless nephew in charge of his operation before he left."

Brooks nodded. "And we've been chipping away at them ever since."

"Evidently Dante is fed up with the good life and is ready to resume command." Once again, Dixon fixed Brooks with his steady regard. "Word is, he's talking pretty big about the cop that shot Lewis."

Brooks felt rather than saw Mike and Donna go rigid. But he just shrugged. Being threatened by punks like Dante was just part of the job. It had never bothered him before, and it didn't now. "Dante was always a big talker."

"Just the same, I want you to watch yourself," Dixon ordered.

"I always do."

With a quick nod, the captain got to his feet and began snapping out orders. "Let's get some real dirt on Wilson soon. Now's the time, before he can build his operation back up again. A lot of people moved in on his business while he was away. Word is, Dante's ordered some hits on some of his competitors. There's some talk of some big deals in the making. And I've got a bad feeling there's going to be some big trouble."

Brooks figured *trouble* was a mild term for the violence that might erupt in the coming weeks. He didn't welcome the tumult, but on the other hand, he felt a familiar exultation. For months now, he and Markowitz had been spinning their wheels on penny-ante stuff. But this was big. It was also dangerous. It was exactly the sort of situation that made anyone involved with a cop very nervous. Which was why so many cops were better off uninvolved.

To his dismay, Brooks spared yet another thought for an auburn beauty with wide brown eyes. Then he pushed Holly MacPherson's image aside.

He, Donna and Mike swung into action, first talking with the undercover cop who had spotted Wilson Saturday night, then fanning out to interview street sources who could further confirm Wilson was in business again. Dixon had made it clear he wanted the top guy this time, and Brooks would be more than happy if he could deliver. Unfortunately, this first day brought him nothing but roadblocks. It seemed no one was ready to say much about Dante Wilson's return to Memphis.

He dragged himself back to the office late that afternoon. And there, among a dozen or so other messages, was one from a Ms. MacPherson. She needed to see him, it said. Tonight.

Wondering just what sort of game she was playing, he first crumpled the pink message slip into a ball and tossed it aside, intent on more-pressing matters. But at six-thirty, when Mike and Donna and even Dixon had gone home, Brooks fished the message out of the wastebasket. There was one way to get to the bottom of this.

Quickly looking up Holly's number, he phoned her. She wasn't home, her grandmother told him, wouldn't be home until after nine when her extended shift ended tonight. The older woman was quite friendly, but she sounded surprised when Brooks said Holly had called him. He frowned, wondering what was up, until the truth hit him.

"Mrs. MacPherson—"

"Nana Flora, please. Everyone calls me that."

"Okay, Nana Flora, you think Zane might be setting me up?"

"I don't..." The woman's words trailed off into a chuckle. "Well, you could be right."

"He probably called. I get so many weird phone calls around here that no one would question a little boy calling and asking me to phone someone else."

"I'm sorry," Nana Flora murmured. "I know he's being a pest."

"He's persistent. I'll say that much for him."

"He likes you."

"But his mother doesn't."

"Oh, that's just Holly." The older woman sighed. "You have to understand. Before Zane was born, she was so hurt. So now she plays it safe. With men like Joel."

Brooks cleared his throat. "Mrs. . . . I mean, Nana Flora, I don't want you to get the wrong impression. I'm not looking . . . I mean, I'm not interested . . . that is to say I don't want . . ." Fumbling for just the right words, he finally just fell silent.

There was a long pause, a cough, then Nana Flora said, "If you're not interested, Lieutenant Casey, then why did you call?"

The telephone receiver seemed to grow hot in Brooks's hand. Or maybe it was his cheek that warmed. He honestly didn't know what to say to the woman. So he avoided an answer and told her a polite but firm goodbye.

He left the office and went out to talk with a few of the contacts he hadn't been able to find during the day. All he got were evasions, and he had exhausted his immediate possibilities well before nine. Later, Brooks liked to think he wouldn't have sought Holly out if he could have gotten a lead on what Dante Wilson might be up to. But that point was moot, since he found himself standing in the E.R. reception area, facing down a disapproving Nurse Coulter while Holly came out from the rear with her purse and jacket.

The way she looked at him shook him in ways that a day spent talking to junkies and minor-league dealers hadn't. He was already feeling like a first-class fool before he explained, "I'd like to talk. About Zane. He called me today."

He expected a protest, a put-off, a polite dismissal. He expected anything but her softly spoken "Then maybe we should talk. Over coffee."

Chapter Three

"For some reason, my little boy has picked you to hero-worship."

"And you're not thrilled, are you?"

With one hand around her mug of coffee, Holly sat back in her chair and studied the man across the narrow table. Brooks Casey looked as tired as she felt. His broad shoulders were drooping a bit beneath his blue chambray shirt, and his eyes were red, as if he had rubbed them repeatedly. He'd ordered a ham-and-cheese omelet from the menu of the diner just down the street from the hospital. Instead of woofing it down as she had expected, he was just toying with the food. And maybe it was the weariness that made him seem so much more approachable tonight. For whatever reason, he hadn't come across like a Neanderthal, as he had on Friday evening. She liked the change. But liking him was even more disturbing than being aggravated by him.

"Holly?" he prompted, a faint smile warming his blue eyes.

She really wished he wasn't so very attractive when he smiled. It kept distracting her, so she looked down at her coffee. "It's not that I don't think you're hero material."

"Is that so?"

Holly glanced up and into his warm eyes once more, then quickly looked away again, forcibly keeping her mind on what she wanted to say. "I think you're probably a very nice person, else you wouldn't have been so kind to Zane from the beginning."

"But..."

"But," she echoed, grinning at him, too. "I don't understand this fixation Zane has with you. I mean, you met him briefly last week and then brought him home when he showed up at your office." She made a dismissive gesture when he started to protest. "I know the reason Zane gave for what he did. But it still just boggles my mind that he's so upset about the prospect of Joel becoming part of our family that he would develop this obsession with you."

Brooks's forehead creased. "Isn't 'obsession' a little strong?"

"You wouldn't think so if you had been at our house this weekend. It was 'Brooks' this and 'Brooks' that. Every other word Zane uttered was about you. You would think the two of you had known each other forever."

"Haven't you ever felt that way about someone?"

"Well, maybe—"

"Some people just hit it off, you know. They have this instant affinity. Isn't that how most friendships start?"

"But Zane's just a little boy, and it isn't exactly friendship he wants," she protested, then bit her lip. She hadn't intended to discuss exactly what Zane said he wanted.

But Brooks put it into one succinct sentence. "He wants us to get together."

"He isn't even clear on what that means."

"But he thinks he is."

"Yes, but—"

"But it isn't possible."

"Of course not." Holly hesitated, not wanting to insult the man, who had been so pleasant so far tonight.

He laughed. "It's okay, Holly. You don't have to tiptoe around me. You're not interested in me. It's no big deal. I'm not interested in you, either."

She had no idea why his careless words caused her such a pang. She flushed, more peeved at her reaction than at him. "Well, I'm glad about that. Nana Flora thought...I mean...even I thought after the other night when you were so..."

"Obnoxious," he supplied before taking a sip of coffee.

She paused to clear her throat. "'Obnoxious' is one way of putting it."

He reached out and touched her forearm where it rested against the tabletop. His fingertips were rough against her skin, and his touch distracted her almost as much as his smile had moments ago. Blinking down at his hand, then up at him, Holly swallowed hard.

But Brooks didn't seem to notice her discomfiture. His expression was quite sincere. "I'm sorry about the other night," he told her. "I was obnoxious. I got real personal about your relationship with Joel. It's a bad habit some cops have. We get in a situation, and we start probing for answers, and we stop considering that we might be overstepping some boundaries. I was way over the line Friday night."

"You did take me by surprise."

"By acting like a Neanderthal?"

She moved her arm away from his touch. "You could say that."

"I'm sorry. I don't know what got into me. Except maybe that I was surprised when you said you and Joel hadn't—" He broke off the last words and gave her a weak smile. "Sorry. There I go. Overstepping again."

Holly chose to ignore his slip. "About Zane," she murmured, attempting to bring the conversation back to its original intent.

"You're afraid he's going to be majorly disappointed when nothing happens between us."

"Maybe that sounds like I'm overreacting, but I know my son and he's acting strange about this. It's almost like he's on a mission of sorts. He actually suggested that I call you up and invite you for dinner last night. He went up to his room and sulked all night when I said no."

"Kids do get worked up about things."

She lifted an eyebrow at his knowing tone.

"I'm the oldest in a big family, remember? At our house, someone was always worked up about something."

"And you got called on to set things right all the time?"

"Yeah. Mom and Dad were great, but just keeping food on the table was a big job. As the oldest, I had a lot of responsibility for the younger kids. I was chief referee, protector and adviser."

She could see how that would happen with eight youngsters to keep up with. "Sounds like you've been a cop your whole life."

He laughed. "I never really thought about it, but I guess you're right. This is really all I ever wanted to do." Turning, he gestured to the waitress for more coffee. "No one else in the family is a cop, that's for sure."

"Then what do they do?"

The waitress refilled their coffee mugs, and Brooks gave Holly the lowdown on his family. His love for them and his pride in their accomplishments were obvious as he talked. She wondered if he realized what a warm, special family portrait his words and expression painted. His mother still worked as a secretary. His sister and her husband had joined his father in the plumbing business. Another sister was a full-time wife and mother. Another taught kindergarten. His twin sisters were both professional women—one a lawyer and the other in banking. His twin brothers were just finishing college.

"Two sets of twins." Holly shook her head, considering the chaos that must have ensued on an average day in that house.

"Twins run in the family. My sister who teaches is due to deliver a set in a couple of months."

"I thought twins were supposed to skip a generation."

"They're in every generation on both sides of my family."

"Wow," she marveled. "The person who marries you had better be ready for any possibility."

"Maybe that's why I'm not married."

"But coming from such a big, terrific family, it seems as if you'd want one of your own."

Chuckling again, he said, "To think that, you *must* be an only child who never had to share a bathroom with seven siblings."

"I expect you *know* I'm an only child. Nana Flora told me you interrogated her about me the other night."

He had the grace to look shamefaced. "Sorry about that."

"I guess you're forgiven," she returned, smiling. "And speaking as an only child who had a bathroom all to myself as well as two doting grandparents, I sort of envy your family. I certainly never wanted Zane to be an only child, too."

"There's still time to remedy that."

Murmuring a vague agreement, she looked down at her coffee. Over the past couple of months, she had come to the conclusions that she would marry Joel and they would give Zane some siblings. She definitely wanted more children. In fact, she wanted something that approximated Brooks's family. Maybe not that large, but with several children who could grow up together, who would love and stand by each other, who would always know that no matter what other differences there might be, there was someone in the world who came from the same place they did.

Maybe she had idealized family life, but she thought the ideal was one worth working toward. She also knew that a good family started with two people who were right for one another. Her grandparents had shown her that much. And she was beginning to realize she hadn't found that man. Maybe that conclusion was due to Zane's attitude about Joel or her own reluctance to become more intimate with him. Perhaps if she allowed herself to move to the next level of intimacy, as Joel was pressing her to do, she would be certain he was the person with whom she could spend the rest of her life. Perhaps her doubts would disappear. But right now she couldn't even imagine making love with Joel. So what did that say? If the possibility was unthinkable, then what would the reality be? Of course, she didn't believe marriage was all about sex, but without that deep, elemental yearning for one another, did two people stand a chance at happiness?

"Something wrong?" Brooks asked.

She cleared her thoughts with a shake of her head. "Sorry. I was daydreaming."

"About having more children?"

"Sort of."

"Is that what Joel wants?"

She moved around in her seat, not sure how she wanted to answer. Despite the congenial nature of the conversation she and Brooks were now having, he had been know-it-all obnoxious Friday night, and she could just imagine his smugness if he thought his questions about her and Joel's relationship had caused her to reconsider what she wanted. His questions weren't the only reason she was reconsidering. And she owed no explanations to a man who was only a little more than a stranger. They were here to talk about Zane, anyway. Why was it their conversation kept veering off in all directions?

"About Zane," she said again.

To Brooks's credit, he followed her lead. "Why don't I talk to him?"

"I'm not sure that's the solution. If you spend time with him, isn't that just going to encourage this little fantasy he's having about you becoming his dad?"

"Not if I talk to him straight."

"I've talked to him straight."

"But you're his mom," Brooks argued, his grin reappearing. "I'm sure Zane believes he can cajole his way into getting you to do just about anything."

"You make him sound like a little con artist."

"From what I've seen, most kids get their parents' number in the first eighteen months. From then on, getting along is just a matter of who gets the jump on whom."

She had to laugh, because that was exactly the way Zane often made her feel. "You really do understand kids."

"So I can talk to him?"

"Okay," she agreed after only a moment's hesitation.

"I'll just explain things. I'll tell him he's a great kid, you're a nice woman, but that Joel—"

Holly broke in, "There's really no need to talk to Zane about Joel."

A wrinkle appeared between Brooks's eyebrows. "Don't you want Zane encouraged to look at Joel as his future father?"

"Well . . . not . . . not exactly."

Brooks eased back in his seat. He opened his mouth as if he was about to ask her something, then reconsidered.

But she felt as if she owed him some sort of explanation, even if it wasn't the whole truth. "As I mentioned the other night, Joel and I haven't decided how serious we are."

"I know that's what you said, but after I met Joel, I thought you'd been putting me on."

"What do you mean?"

"Just that I got the impression things were a little more serious than you had said."

Thinking of the way she had hung on to Joel on the front porch, Holly began to feel foolish. "Why would I lie?"

Brooks raised an eyebrow. "I'm probably overstepping again, but the man gave me the impression that he was pretty far gone about you. And he seemed really concerned about Zane not liking him."

"Just because he cares and he wants Zane to like him doesn't mean we're getting married."

"Then what are you doing?"

"Dating."

"And he has no expectations?"

"No . . . I mean, yes, he does. . . ."

"So it's you that has the problem. You don't know how you feel."

"I do care for Joel, but..." Blowing out a frustrated breath, Holly glared at Brooks. "But I don't want to discuss this with you."

Eyes narrowed, he studied her for a moment. Then he reached for the check the waitress had left, and when he spoke again it was about Zane. "I'll call you or his grandmother and set up a time to come talk to him."

She nodded, distracted from thoughts of Zane. Brooks's cool tone bothered her almost as much as his avid interest had earlier. She didn't want to analyze why she kept having this schizo reaction to him. What she wanted, at this moment, was to get away from him—far away.

But she kept noticing little things about him as they vacated their booth. The easy way he shrugged into his worn bomber jacket. The generous tip he left for the waitress. The friendly smile he had for the cashier. The way he held the door open and insisted on walking her to her car. The firm, masculine line of his jaw when he tipped his head back and pointed to the yellow moon hovering high over the Memphis skyline.

"Look at that," he murmured. "An Elvis moon."

"What?"

He laughed rather self-consciously. "A full moon is called an Elvis moon in my family."

"I'm almost afraid to ask why."

"It's silly, I guess. But my folks moved here to Memphis just after they married. It was summer and really hot, and at night when they couldn't sleep they used to come down and walk near the river where it was cooler. One night, when there was a full moon,

they got a little romantic. But then someone interrupted them.''

"Elvis?" Holly asked, sensing the direction of the
story.

"Yeah. My father says he acted real embarrassed at
having stumbled on them, but he was nice, too. Even
gave them his autograph. My folks have it framed and
hanging in the family room at home. And from that
night on, they've called every full moon an Elvis
moon. It's a family tradition.''

Holly leaned against her car door, gazing up at the
sky. "It's a nice tradition.''

"And you're..."

She glanced at Brooks as his words trailed away.
"I'm what?''

He shook his head, then took a step forward, so
close to her that she could feel the warmth coming off
his solid male frame. She was tall compared to a lot of
women, but she had to look up to face Brooks. And
she did look up, into eyes cast in shadows by the lights
streaming from the diner. She couldn't read his expression in the dark, but his body language spoke
volumes.

"What is it?" she repeated softly, although she already knew.

He kissed her. With a smoothness born of experience. With a hesitancy that was even more beguiling.
But as Holly responded, hesitance fled, replaced by a
sizzle that reached down inside her and seemed to lift
her up, the same way his strong arms lifted her off
the ground. It was a lips-opening, bodies-grinding-
together sort of kiss. Not at all like Holly thought a
proper first kiss should be. But that thought quickly

faded. Everything faded but the feel of Brooks's arms around her, his mouth against her lips, against her jaw, her neck.

As if from a long distance, Holly heard herself whispering his name. Brokenly. Breathlessly. She hardly recognized the voice as her own. And maybe that's what made her pull away. Brooks let her go without protest. And then they stood, both breathing hard, just staring at one another.

Finally, Holly managed to begin a sentence of explanation. "I don't know—"

"But I do know," Brooks interrupted. "I know you don't give a damn about that accountant."

Her mouth flew open. "But I . . . I . . ."

He stepped close again, his big hand cupping her chin. Slowly, he smoothed his thumb across her lower lip. She was immobilized by the confusing wave of yearning that rushed through her. Then Brooks kissed her again. A short, hard, thoroughly bone-melting kiss. For the space of a heartbeat, he leaned his forehead against hers. Then he left, striding across the parking lot toward his car without looking back.

Holly got quickly behind the wheel of her own car. But she didn't start the engine. She sat, one hand pressed to the lips Brooks had kissed so well. It was several minutes before she gathered enough energy to turn the key and pull out of the parking lot.

And perhaps it was her imagination, but she could have sworn the Elvis moon winked at her all the way home.

Dumb.
Dumber.

Dumbest.

Those were the only words that seemed to fit as Brooks considered the events of the night. As the hour neared eleven o'clock and crept past, he sat at his desk idly tapping a pencil against a blank legal pad. Though the precinct hummed with activity on the floors below him, up here it was quiet and nearly deserted. Offices all around his were darkened for the night. There was nothing to distract him from the memory of Holly in his arms. Her scent. Her taste. Her husky voice repeating his name.

God, but he had been dumb to go see her. Dumber to go out for coffee and conversation. But the dumbest move of all had been kissing her. He hadn't intended anything of the sort. But there she stood, her face tipped up in the moonlight, looking so sweet, so kissable. And he went with his instincts.

Dumb move.

She wasn't for him. For all the reasons he had already considered, the two of them had no possibility of any kind of relationship. From a man, she wanted a family and promises of forever. From a woman, he wanted only sex and some lighthearted companionship. Holly needed to stick with her safe and secure accountant. Brooks needed to find an outlet for the sexual urges muddying his thinking. Only there was no way a woman as honest and decent as Holly could remain with the accountant if she could kiss Brooks as she had. And every sexual thought he'd been having—and there'd been at least a hundred in the hour since he'd left her—centered around a long-legged, auburn-haired nurse with eyes like dark chocolate and lips like honey.

Hell, she even had him thinking in romantic clichés.

Brooks pushed away from his desk with a vicious oath, got up and strode to the coffeemaker, where half a pot of industrial-strength brew was waiting. He had just filled his chipped, stained mug when Mike strode into the office.

Mike paused for a second, looking surprised to see Brooks. "Is something up?"

"Not with me," Brooks answered. "What are you doing here?"

Shrugging, Mike tossed his jacket down on his desk and got his own mug. "Thought I'd get a little work done."

"Little late for that, isn't it?"

"So what? You're here."

Brooks had worked with Mike too long to be put off by his crisp tone. Without saying another word to the plump, balding detective, he went back to his desk and pretended to be making a list. He couldn't help noticing, however, that Mike was in an edgy mood—pacing, sitting down and getting up, opening and closing drawers, mumbling under his breath.

Eventually, as Brooks knew he would, Mike said, "Man, I gotta talk."

"Sure." Brooks laid aside his pad and pen. "I figured something must be wrong for you to be here this time of night."

Mike chewed on his upper lip for a minute, his gaze centered somewhere over Brooks's head. "Me and Patty aren't going to make it."

Something in his expression made Brooks resist offering the platitudes that sprang to his lips. "I'm sorry," was all he said.

"Twenty-three years." Mike sighed. "And I've been a cop for twenty of 'em. And we've been through so much. Money troubles. The kids." He shook his head. "But now?"

"Now she doesn't know if she can take it anymore. She hates the phone calls late at night, the unpredictable hours, the weekends when I've got to follow up a lead." Mike shook his head. "She says that after years of watching me walk out the door every morning and wondering if that's the day some lunatic turns a gun on me, she just can't keep doing it."

Because he knew his friend was really suffering, Brooks chose his words carefully. "Would it help if you transferred?"

Mike folded his arms across his ample stomach and said nothing.

Brooks continued. "What if you got a different assignment? Something with fewer risks?"

"Would you be happy with that?"

"We're not talking about me."

"But we're a lot alike, you and me." Getting up, Mike shoved his hands in the pockets of his jeans and began to pace. "You and me and Donna, we all like the edginess of this job. Look at today, how we all came alive when we heard Dante was back on the scene. We knew something big was about to explode, so we were up. Living with the risks isn't easy, but I don't know if living without them would be any easier."

"Would you rather live without Patty?"

Brooks's quiet question made Mike stop. His face was averted, and whatever emotions might have been revealed there were wiped clean before he turned around. "I don't know," he murmured. "Brooks, buddy, I just don't know."

There wasn't much more Brooks could say. But the agony Mike and Patty DeWitt were living through just underscored how right Brooks was to stay away, far away, from Holly. No matter how good it had felt to kiss her.

Mike suddenly rubbed his hands together. "Hey, man, I know it's late and it's a work night, but how about a beer?"

Drinking his troubles away had never been high on Brooks's or Mike's agenda. But the thought of a cold brew in a loud, smoky room was appealing right now.

"Let's go down on Beale," Brooks suggested, referring to Memphis's famous street where the blues had been born. "Maybe we'll find some music sad enough to accompany our problems."

Taking up his jacket again, Mike agreed, though he added, "You, my friend, are unmarried. Therefore, you have no real concept of the word 'problems.'"

Brooks clapped his friend on the shoulder as they headed out the door. "Keep reminding me about that, buddy. Believe me, I need to keep hearing it." *Especially with Holly's kiss still fresh on my lips.*

Tapping lightly at the door to her grandmother's room, Holly murmured. "Nana, you awake?"

"Of course."

Holly pushed the door open and smiled at the older woman, who was propped up in bed, reading. Even at seventy-one, Nana Flora made a pretty picture against the lace-trimmed pillow cases, surrounded by the soft glow of her bedside lamp. "I saw your light was still on when I came up the stairs."

Nana Flora set her book down on the flower-sprigged comforter and peered at Holly over her spectacles. "I heard you come in a while ago. What have you been doing?"

"Drinking a pot of herb tea and thinking about Brooks Casey."

Mouth forming a silent "Oh," Nana Flora gave Holly a long look, then patted the bed beside her. "So he called you."

"We went for coffee and talked about Zane." Holly sat down next to her grandmother and resisted the urge to lay her head in the woman's lap as she used to do when she was a child in need of comfort and advice.

"And what happened?"

"He kissed me."

Nana Flora compressed her lips, obviously hiding a smile. "Well, that's no crime."

"It was wonderful." Holly hated admitting that, but she had to talk about it or lose her mind.

"There's nothing tragic about a wonderful kiss, is there?"

"There is when you're not kissing the right man."

"How do you know he's not right?"

"Because he can't be," Holly protested, getting up and pacing to the ruffled-curtain-draped window. "He's a cop, for God's sake."

Nana Flora went very still.

Turning away, Holly squeezed her eyes shut, berating herself for her impulsive words before she whirled back to face her grandmother. "I'm sorry. I didn't mean that to sound so dismissive."

"Your grandfather would be ashamed of you," Nana Flora said stiffly, very carefully removing her glasses. "Police work is honorable, important work."

"And it's underappreciated and underpaid, and policemen are overworked and overburdened. You and I know that all too well."

"We also know that what a person does is so often a part of who they are." The older woman pushed herself up, shifting the pillows behind her back into a more comfortable position. "It's like you," she told Holly. "Would you be the nurse that you are if you didn't care so much for others, if you didn't really want to make a difference in the lives of people who are ill?"

"I've seen good nurses who aren't so empathetic."

"Good but not exceptional."

Holly looked away, knowing the woman who had raised her was right, as usual. "None of this has anything to do with Brooks or what happened tonight."

"Well, to have kissed him, you must have seen something in him that you liked or admired."

Holly had to chuckle. "Oh, Nana, you've got such a pure heart. Maybe my kissing him had nothing at all to do with his character."

Nana Flora laughed, as well. "I wasn't born yesterday, Holly Veronica MacPherson. And I will say that, if I was the one doing the choosing and the kissing, I'd much rather kiss Brooks Casey than Joel Preston."

"Nana!"

"I always was partial to big, brawny men."

"Like Papa Jake."

"Just like him." Nana Flora held out her hand to Holly, who sat down on the bed beside her again. "Brooks really reminds me of my Jake."

"He does?" Until that moment, Holly hadn't thought about the physical similarities between the two men, but Nana Flora was right. They were both tall and broad shouldered, big boned and rough edged, with a gruffness that could put people off at first.

"I think he probably reminds Zane of Papa, too."

"But Zane was barely six when Papa Jake died. Surely he doesn't remember that much about him."

"Don't you remember your father?"

Holly thought of the handsome man who used to swing her high in the air till she squealed in gleeful protest. Only three when he died, she could still summon his features to mind, could still hear his deep voice. Maybe it was the love her ill-fated young father had given her that made him so vivid, much more so than the mother who had exited her life without a backward glance. Papa Jake had given that same love to Holly and then to Zane. So of course Zane remembered him.

"Maybe that's why Zane's obsessed with Brooks," she murmured.

"Maybe Zane's smart enough to recognize a good man."

"Joel is a good man."

Nana Flora took hold of her hand. "But after kissing Joel, you never came in here looking all lit up." She lifted gentle, age-roughened fingers to Holly's face. "To my knowledge, Joel's never made you look as alive as you do tonight."

Holly closed her eyes, knowing her grandmother's all-seeing wisdom was on target. Even before Brooks had kissed her, there was something in the air between them. A wave of awareness. An exhilaration. But that didn't change some facts.

"Brooks isn't just a cop," she said, looking at Nana Flora again. "He's undercover, I think. He was on stakeout or something when he had to bring his partner into the hospital and he met up with Zane."

The other woman nodded. "From the way he was dressed Friday night, I gathered he wasn't a mere patrolman."

"He's probably in danger all the time."

"It takes a strong man to live with that."

With a frustrated groan, Holly gave in to her need for comfort and laid her head on her grandmother's chest. "You're determined to shoot down every excuse I have for not seeing this man, aren't you?"

"I'm simply playing devil's advocate."

"You should be *my* advocate."

Nana Flora stroked her hair, chuckling. "If you didn't want my honest opinion, you shouldn't have come in here and told me he kissed you."

"You'd have guessed anyway."

"Probably," her grandmother said smugly. "When are you seeing him again?"

"He's supposed to call, to come and talk to Zane."

"That's good."

Holly remained silent for a moment more. Then she said, "I kissed him back, Nana. I don't think I've ever kissed anyone like that or felt that way. It frightens me a little."

"It'll be fine."

"I just don't want to make another mistake, not like the first time I lost my head over a man—"

"Shh," Nana Flora soothed. "You're a grown-up now, Holly. I know you'll make the right choices."

"I sure hope so. But I'd feel better about it if kissing Brooks didn't turn my head completely around."

In the hall outside Nana Flora's room, Zane clapped a hand over his mouth to keep from expressing his excitement. He crept back to his room, careful to miss the squeaky board in the center of the hall. Only after he had softly closed his door did he lift one arm and bring it sharply down by his side while uttering a quiet but triumphant "Yes!"

His mom had kissed Brooks. And his Nana Flora thought that was good. While Zane wasn't any too sure why adults seemed to enjoy kissing so much, he knew from all the movies he had watched and from observing Charleen and Bob and other parents, that kissing was important. So if Brooks and his mom wanted to kiss, then maybe...

Trying to be quiet so that his mom wouldn't know he was up, he scrambled into bed. From under his pillow, he pulled out the cardboard sword covered in tinfoil that they had made last week at his Knights club meeting. Wondercat jumped onto his bed to watch while Zane lifted the sword high above his head, as he imagined a knight who had completed his quest might do.

Mom had said Brooks would be calling to come and see him. But Zane knew his mother was probably the real attraction. And maybe if she and Brooks kissed again, she would kiss old Joel goodbye forever.

He tucked the sword safely away and snuggled under the covers with a world of pleasant possibilities to hold the darkness of the night at bay.

Chapter Four

The week had been a long series of stone walls and dead ends as far as Brooks was concerned. After days of putting out feelers all over the city, he pulled his car into the precinct parking lot late Friday afternoon with no clue about what Dante Wilson was up to. Brooks had an elusive, uncomfortable feeling the man was out there somewhere, laughing as the police circled their wagons and waited for him to appear.

"Maybe Dante's not really in town," Markowitz, who was riding in the passenger's seat, suggested.

Brooks grunted. His young partner had returned to the office on Tuesday. After a couple of days of desk work, he had come on board the Dante investigation today, but he had been one big zero when it came to help.

Markowitz lifted himself gingerly out of the car, groaning. Brooks tried not to be irritated. He was sure the other man was still in pain from his injury, but hearing about it for hours on end had worn his patience thin. He had to force himself to slow his steps to walk beside Markowitz into the office.

"Seriously," the younger officer continued, "maybe the whole thing is just one big mix-up. The undercover who IDed Dante last weekend was probably wrong. The dealer they nabbed probably lied about Dante in order to divert attention from himself."

Brooks shook his head. "Dante's here," he said gruffly. "I can smell him."

"Smell him?" Markowitz's laughter held an edge of derision. "Is that supposed to be some sort of veteran cop's trick? Will I be able to *smell* the bad guys someday?"

It was all Brooks could do to keep from snapping at his companion as they made their way through the chaotic precinct receiving area. A crowd of uniformed officers milled around the front desk, as well as several citizens and even a couple of media people that Brooks recognized. Therefore, he kept his voice level and his tone pleasant. "Call it a trick or call it instinct. I just know he's back in town. Every time I mention his name, I see a look in people's eyes. Fear. Dante's back and he's going to cause trouble."

"Maybe people are just afraid because they know you killed Dante's son."

Brooks didn't know if Markowitz had intended his voice to carry so well, or if that was an accident. Whatever the case, the result was most of the conversation around them silenced. Brooks could feel stares boring into him before a throat was cleared, phones began to ring and the normal precinct sounds swelled again. Turning on his heel, he left Markowitz behind and took the stairs two at a time to the second floor.

He was standing by the clerk's desk at the top of the stairs, shifting angrily through his messages, when Markowitz limped off the elevator.

"Listen, Casey, I didn't mean . . ."

Not even looking up, Brooks gave Markowitz's fumbling attempt at an apology no encouragement.

"This has just been a bad time, you know. I mean, first this stupid injury. And . . . well . . . I'm in pain here, man."

Brooks finally glanced up. "Yeah, I know you are. I know *exactly* how it feels to ride around all day with a pain in the ass."

Markowitz's fair skin flushed crimson. "Now, look—"

"No, you look," Brooks retorted, losing his cool completely. "If I were at your stage in my career, and I had the chance to be in on bringing down a major leaguer like Dante, I would be a little more into it than you appear to be. I'd be trying to come up with some suggestions, some leads, some plan of action. I'd certainly be trying to use the contacts you are supposed to have on the streets to find out what's going on."

"I have the contacts," Markowitz broke in. "But can you honestly say you'd listen to me?"

"I might if you didn't spend your time crying over an injury that was your own damn fault."

"That's low, Casey."

"No, it was dumb, Markowitz. About as dumb as you pissing off the man—me—who's assigned to cover you if you get caught in a jam."

To Brooks's surprise, Markowitz didn't back down. "Maybe things would be different if my partner didn't brush me off like an annoying fly—"

"When that's the way you act—"

"Casey! Markowitz!" Dixon's voice sliced through the air. "What's the problem?"

Markowitz didn't stick around to hear what else the captain had to say. With a muffled curse, he stalked back toward the stairs.

Brooks snorted. "Well, look at that, he forgot to limp."

Wavering for only a moment, Markowitz banged the door to the staircase open. It hit against the wall like a cannon shot, echoing long after the detective had disappeared from view.

Arms crossed on his massive chest, Dixon demanded, "What the hell was that all about?"

"His butt hurts," Brooks quipped.

The pretty young clerk, who was relatively new on the job and had watched the confrontation between partners with wide eyes, giggled. Dixon glared at her, and she wheeled to answer a ringing telephone. Then the captain focused on Brooks again. "Can't you and Markowitz get along for one day? He just came off sick leave, and you're already at each other's throats."

"I've told you before. I don't want a partner. Especially not that kid."

"And I told you—too bad."

"Lieutenant." The clerk's voice broke into their exchange. She held up the telephone. "It's for you, Lieutenant Casey. Line four. That little boy again."

"What little boy?"

"The one who has called every day this week."

Zane MacPherson. Brooks groaned as realization struck. He had a stack of messages from Zane this week, but he had decided talking to Holly's son would be just one more in a series of dumb moves. "Take a message."

Darting an anxious look at Captain Dixon, the clerk pursed her lips, then cleared her throat. "But, Lieutenant Casey, he's called every single day this week."

"I said take a message."

"But, sir—"

"For God's sake, Casey," Dixon growled. "Take the damn call. This woman isn't your personal answering service." He stalked away, jerking the door to his office shut behind him.

Brooks glowered at the clerk, who held up four fingers. "Line four."

Grumbling, he went to his desk and punched the line with a vicious swipe. "Casey here."

"Hiya, Brooks."

The sound of that young, hopeful voice was like a bucket of cold water on Brooks's temper. After a day spent talking to weirdos and losers, it was especially refreshing to hear from a kid like Zane. A kid whose tenaciousness Brooks had to grudgingly admire. He had no business liking this kid, but damn it, he did. Passing a hand over his face, he said, "Hey there, Zane."

"Mom said you might be calling me."

"I know, little man. I'm sorry I haven't."

"Nana Flora says you're probably real busy."

Thinking of all the roadblocks he had run into this week, Brooks nodded grimly, but all he said was, "Your nana's right."

"She's making spaghetti for dinner tonight."

"One of your favorites?"

"Her spaghetti is awesome. You should come eat with us."

"I couldn't just show up, you know. That wouldn't be polite."

"But I'm inviting you."

"Now, Zane—"

"It's okay, really," the little boy explained. "Mom lets me have a friend over for dinner on Friday nights most of the time. I said I wanted you to come."

So Holly knew he was being asked to dinner. That surprised Brooks. After the other night, he had figured she wouldn't want him coming around her son. She might have kissed him back, but she had made it clear she wasn't interested. Hell, he wasn't interested in her, either. Not in anything but the most prurient sense, which meant, of course, that he might as well forget it.

"Please."

The little boy's plea tugged at Brooks's resolve. After the week he'd had, the last thing he needed was to expose himself to Holly's particular brand of charm. But saying no to her son was much more difficult than he would have dreamed only moments ago.

Letting out a long sigh, he said, "What time's dinner?"

"Seven-thirty, 'cause we're waiting on Mom to come home and eat with us. Can you come?"

"I'll try." Zane's excited cheer nearly deafened Brooks. He held the receiver away from his ear until the boy quieted. "But if I'm not there, don't wait to eat."

"Okay, but try. Try really hard." Without even a goodbye, Zane slammed down the phone.

Brooks replaced the receiver and rocked back in his chair, disgusted with himself. Now he had done it. Gone and gotten the boy's hopes up. What a coward he was. It would have been much better to keep avoiding Zane until he gave up.

Or would it?

Rubbing his chin thoughtfully, Brooks considered his options. What he wanted most was to avoid Holly, but he had promised her he would talk to Zane. Not following through on an obligation was no example to set for the boy. Despite what had happened with Holly, Brooks could still see Zane tonight, have a talk with him, make him see that Brooks wasn't a father candidate. He could go early, before Holly came home, and he could excuse himself before dinner. He might not even have to see her. That was great, just great.

So why wasn't he smiling? Why, against all his better judgment, did he *want* to see Holly? Maybe she wanted to see him, too? Why else would she let Zane call and invite him? Maybe that kiss had been even more potent than he suspected.

"Bad news?" The clerk dropped some papers into the basket on Brooks's desk, diverting his thoughts.

"What?"

"You look like you got bad news. From the little boy?"

Brooks made a dismissive gesture. "No, not really."

"Oh, well..." The clerk—Julie was her name, Brooks thought—continued just to stand by his desk.

"Something else you need?"

Her peaches-and-cream complexion flushed a delicate pink. "No, nothing, I guess..." She touched her hand to her stylishly tousled mane of blond hair and smoothed down the snug black skirt that covered her slender hips. *Her slender but curvaceous hips.*

Suddenly reading her body language, Brooks swallowed hard. It wasn't like him to be struck dumb in the face of a woman sending off obvious signals of interest, but he honestly couldn't think of a thing to say.

She smiled as she leaned against his desk. "I was just wondering if you could...if *we* could maybe have a drink or something some night. I'm working as a clerk right now, but I'm really interested in police work."

Brooks recovered some of his normal poise. "Is that so?"

"And I thought you might be willing to tell me what it's really like to be on the force."

"Aren't you picking up on what it's really like just by working here?"

Her blue eyes widened. "Well, yes, I am. But for an insider's view...well, everyone says you've seen it all, Lieutenant Casey. That you've worked on so many big cases."

"Well..." Brooks didn't know what in the world was wrong with him. Here was a beautiful woman, flattering him, asking him out. A month ago, weeks ago, he would have taken her up on her offer without hesitation. They would have gone for that drink and then probably dinner, and if the chemistry remained intact, they might have wound up at her place, or his. And perhaps with her, he could have found a release for the sexual tension that had curled him into knots ever since he had kissed Holly on Monday night.

With a coquettish flutter of her long, dark lashes, Julie leaned forward. "Are you busy tonight? Maybe we could go have that talk."

Brooks wanted to feel a response to her. A response he had counted on since he was eleven and realized that from his window he could see his pretty sixteen-year-old neighbor getting dressed in her bedroom next door. But as he looked up at Julie, at her full, slightly parted lips, at the rounded swell of her breasts beneath her fuzzy pink sweater, Brooks felt not one stir of sexual arousal. And that was a hell of note. What was wrong with him?

"How about it?" Julie asked.

He let out a sigh. "I'm sorry. I've already got plans."

She pouted prettily. "Maybe some other time."

"Maybe."

"Okay." She walked away, smiling at him over her shoulder as she passed Mike and Donna coming in the door.

Donna lifted one eyebrow. Mike turned to watch Julie's hips sway and pretended to wipe perspiration off his forehead. Brooks held up his hands, as if to fend off their comments. "Don't start with me, guys."

"As long as you're not starting anything with anyone else." Donna nodded toward the glassed wall beyond which Julie was visible at her desk.

"Don't worry," Brooks grumbled. "I've got bigger problems than even that."

Mike dropped into his desk chair. "Like what?"

"Like dinner with a nine-year-old." Brooks stood and picked up his jacket. "A nine-year-old and his mother." There, he'd said it. Now there needn't be any more pretense about avoiding Holly, even to himself.

Interest gleamed in Donna's eyes. "The nurse and her kid?"

"Holly and Zane MacPherson."

Groaning, Mike laid his head on his desk. "You're screwed, man."

"No, I'm not," Brooks retorted. "Nor am I likely to be tonight or anytime in the near future."

He ducked the paper wad Donna threw at him, then spared one more glance at Julie, who was talking on the phone, her little black skirt hiked high enough to reveal the long length of her slender, crossed legs. She caught him looking and grinned.

Turning his back on his smirking friends, Brooks walked past the young clerk with only a curt goodbye. He was going home early to have a shower and get changed for dinner with Zane.

Dinner with Holly.

As he pushed through the door Markowitz had slammed open only a short while before, Brooks found himself imagining Holly in the same skirt Julie was wearing. And the arousal he had wanted earlier came to him quickly. With all the intensity he had always taken for granted.

And it shook him. Because this was the first time in Brooks Casey's adult life that sexual arousal was focused on just one woman, a whole woman—not just her attractive face or tantalizing smile or curvy figure. Hell, he used to get excited just standing in a crowded elevator smelling a stranger's perfume. But for days, whenever he looked at any woman, he had found himself wishing he were looking at Holly. Just Holly. And it hadn't taken thoughts of a tight skirt and sweater to get him going.

He tried to tell himself everything would be fine, that this was a temporary obsession, that nothing in his free-wheeling romantic life had changed for good. But he couldn't. Not now.

And certainly not hours later, when he watched Holly MacPherson walk into her living room.

Instead of a short skirt, she wore a rumpled uniform. Her shoulder-length hair was tousled, but not stylishly. And instead of a welcoming smile, her expression was a mixture of Friday-night weariness and surprise. Yet Brooks thought she was infinitely more beautiful than the young clerk who had put a move on him earlier.

He wanted her.

The need slammed into him with all the subtlety of a wrecking ball. He wanted to touch Holly, hold her, grind his lips across hers, feel her body moving against his. And he wanted even more than that. He longed just to sit with her, hold her hand, catch her smiles and talk. That's right. Just talk.

Mike was right, Brooks decided.

He was screwed.

* * *

Holly closed the dishwasher door and stood for a moment in the kitchen, listening to the little-boy laughter and deep, rumbly chuckles coming from the living room.

"I don't know who's having a better time with that video game, Brooks or Zane," said Nana Flora. She was busy working on a hem in the kitchen alcove she used as a sewing room.

Murmuring a noncommittal reply, Holly turned to give the counter a last, unnecessary swipe with the damp dishrag.

"Isn't it about Zane's bedtime?" her grandmother added.

"There's no school tomorrow."

"But wouldn't you like him to go to bed, so you could talk to Brooks?"

Holly shot Nana Flora a warning glance as she hung up the rag. "He came to talk to Zane."

"They talked before you ever got here. Talked all through dinner."

"That doesn't mean they can't talk now, too."

"Brooks is just hanging around now, waiting for you to stop hiding in the kitchen. Since when does it take you an hour to clean up in here?"

"I'm not hiding. I had a rough day at work, and I'm moving kind of slow." Holly winced as sore muscles protested her quick movements. Work had actually been more than rough, but she didn't want to think about that now.

Nana Flora sniffed. "Brooks came over to see you just as much as Zane."

"We don't know that."

"Oh, for pity's sake." The older woman glared over her spectacles at Holly. "Don't be obtuse, Holly. This is Friday night, and a man like Brooks doesn't have to spend Friday with a nine-year-old, no matter how much he likes him. Get out there and talk to him. You've waited all week for him to call."

Holly stiffened. "I have not."

"So why else have you been jumping for the phone like a jackrabbit?

"I don't know what you're talking about." It bothered Holly that her grandmother noticed she had been waiting for Brooks to call. She should have known he wouldn't, of course, even after kissing her. Brooks Casey was probably the sort of carelessly flirtatious man who kissed most every woman who let him. A lot of cops were that way, she thought, probably because they had to meet so many people, talk to them, often charm them into talking. She knew all about charming cops.

Beyond that, Brooks was a young, virile man. And that kiss they shared had sizzled. So he had probably shown up here tonight, not just to talk to Zane, but in hopes that Holly was going to do something more than kiss him. Well, he was out of luck. Flat out of luck.

Wasn't he?

The tiny edge of doubt creeping into her resolve irritated Holly even more than Nana Flora.

And the older woman wasn't through. "If you don't want to spend any time with Brooks," she said, grinning, "just why did you change into that outfit?"

Puzzled, Holly looked down at the casual dark green leggings and matching sweater she wore. "What's wrong with this?"

"It's brand-new. Since when do you sit around on a Friday night in something brand-new?"

Coloring and thrusting her chin in the air, Holly poured herself a second cup of coffee, then pushed open the door to the hallway and followed the sounds of males at play. To her dismay, however, a nervous tingle attacked her midsection as soon as she saw Brooks sprawled out with Zane on the living room floor in front of the television set. At this angle, it was impossible for Holly not to notice and appreciate the tight fit of Brooks's worn blue jeans across his muscular thighs and trim rear end.

She started to think about what Nana Flora had said—that Brooks had come to see Holly as much as Zane. The older woman was right—he had called just when Holly had begun to think he wouldn't. The nervous tingle turned into an out-and-out flutter. He had called and he was here.

Catching sight of Holly, Zane demanded, "Is it time for bed, Mom?"

"Not quite."

The boy cocked his head toward the clock on the fireplace mantel. "It's nearly ten."

Holly frowned. This was the first time since Zane had learned to tell time that he had actually reminded her of a bedtime.

"What's the matter?" Brooks got to his knees and ruffled the boy's hair. "Afraid I'm going to beat you again?"

"No way, but—" Covering his mouth with his hand, Zane gave a king-size yawn. "I am kind of tired."

"Are you getting sick?" Holly murmured, crossing the room.

Zane ducked away from her outstretched hand. "I'm fine, Mom. Just tired." He pivoted toward the foyer, a grin splitting his face from ear to ear. "I think I'm gonna go on up to bed."

Beside Holly, Brooks stood and addressed the boy. "You remember what we talked about, okay?"

The youngster's smile deepened. "Sure thing, Brooks."

Holly was beginning to feel she was being had. "I'll come up and tuck you in," she told Zane.

"I'm not a baby," he protested.

As if on cue, Nana Flora appeared in the foyer beside him, her yawn just as elaborate as the boy's had been. "I'm going up, too. I'll make sure he brushes his teeth." With quick good-nights for Brooks and Holly, the senior citizen and nine-year-old disappeared side by side up the stairs.

Glaring after them, Holly muttered, "Conspirators."

"What?"

She turned to find Brooks standing close by, thumbs hooked in the waistband of those obscenely well-fitting jeans as he grinned at her.

"Nothing," she said, hastily backing away. She held up her mug. "Could I offer you some more coffee or something?"

"Not a thing." After switching off the video game, he stood in the center of the room.

The only polite thing for Holly to do was gesture for him to sit down. He courteously waited until she sat on one end of the sofa then joined her at the other end.

That might not have been such a problem, except that it wasn't a large couch to begin with, and Brooks was a big man. Holly felt as if he was crowding her. Or maybe the problem was that she was so very attuned to his every movement.

"Nice room," he said after the silence in the room had stretched to an uncomfortable point.

She grabbed hold of the subject for all it was worth, giving him a rundown on the house, which her grandparents had purchased over forty years ago. She and Nana Flora had done some inexpensive remodeling last year. Just paint and new curtains, mostly, but Holly was proud of the clean lines of this white-walled room with its broad, old-fashioned windows and polished plank flooring. Holly wasn't really aware that she was babbling on about decorating until she caught sight of the crooked grin on Brooks's face. Her voice faded.

Brooks said dryly, "Like I said, nice room."

She took a deep breath. "I'm sorry. I don't usually run on like that unless I'm . . ." She swallowed. "Unless I'm nervous."

He turned sideways, drawing his leg up on the sofa cushions and putting his arm along the back. "Do I make you nervous?"

"A little, I guess."

His grin flashed. "Afraid I might kiss you again?"

Afraid he would or wouldn't? Holly closed her mind on that question and looked away, not sure how to answer him.

"I promise I won't." His voice was soft but gruff. She glanced back at him. "Not unless you want me to."

But she didn't know what she wanted. "Brooks, please, do we have to discuss this?"

"Okay, okay, I'm sorry." He laughed then and stretched with the easy grace of a big, powerful cat. "Do you realize I'm always apologizing to you?"

"Yes." She couldn't resist grinning at him. "Maybe that should tell you something."

"Like what?"

"Like maybe you should learn to behave yourself."

"You make me sound like one of Zane's naughty friends."

She hesitated before replying. "Isn't that what you are? *Zane's* friend."

His blue-eyed gaze was steady on hers. "If that's what you want me to be."

Another question she couldn't answer. "Nana Flora said you and Zane talked for quite a while before I came home tonight. What about?"

"About him not meddling in his mother's love life. Or in mine."

"And he accepted that."

"I'm not sure."

"Why? What'd he do?"

Brooks chuckled again. "That's one crafty little man there. He gave every appearance of agreeing while very skillfully avoiding making any real promises. He's going to make a hell of a politician someday."

She rolled her eyes. "Pardon me if I'm not proud." Turning, she reached for the mug of cooling coffee she had placed on the end table. The twisting movement was just enough to make her sore muscles protest once more, and she groaned.

The cushions of the sofa shifted as Brooks slid closer. "Hey, are you all right?"

She turned again, not altogether surprised to find him now sitting right beside her. She immediately tensed, and her muscles objected again. Managing a grimacing laugh, she explained. "We had a fighter in the E.R. today. It took five of us to hold him down before we could sedate him."

Brooks nodded as if he understood. "Some doper?"

She nodded. "He was just a kid, really. Not more than seventeen or eighteen. Someone had beaten him pretty badly, but he wasn't too thrilled about letting us help him." Pushing up the sleeve of her sweater, she gingerly touched the now purpling bruises on her right arm.

With a low whistle, Brooks took gentle hold of her wrist. "He really got a grip on you, didn't he?"

"I didn't expect him to be so strong. He got hold of me before I could see what was coming." Despite her best intentions, she groaned again as Brooks lifted her arm higher.

His blue eyes widened with concern. "He really hurt you."

"I'm just sore," she protested, trying to ease her arm from him.

But he held her firmly, his long and surprisingly tender fingers pushing her loose sleeve higher. Each inch revealed another, more ugly bruise. She was literally turning black and blue from shoulder to wrist on her right arm. Almost mechanically, she held out her left arm when Brooks asked for it. Here, the bruises were less pronounced but still visible.

"That bastard did more than just grab you," Brooks said, a hint of steel in his deep tone. "What happened?"

"He was quiet when the EMT team brought him in. But the minute I touched him..." Holly couldn't control her shudder, suddenly replaying that moment when the patient had taken hold of her arm. She saw his wild, dilated eyes. Smelled his foul breath. Felt the crusted dirt and blood on his clothes as he jerked her down on top of him. Heard his strangled cries of pain and protest. Heard her own calls for help as she struggled to get away. Remembering the two burly interns it took to pull her away, she sucked in her breath.

Brooks's arm slid immediately around her shoulders. "It's okay," he murmured against her hair. "It's okay."

Aghast at having succumbed to the memory of those tense moments, Holly pulled away from him. Reluctantly so, she realized. There was real comfort in being held so close to his warm, broad chest. Way too much comfort. "I'm sorry. I don't usually act like this."

"But surely it's not every day that some zonked-out kid mauls you."

"It happens," she retorted. "I'm sure you of all people know that it happens."

"But I'm a big guy. I can handle the punks."

She didn't like his implication that she couldn't. It was the same argument she'd had in the beginning of her relationship with Joel, when she had been foolish enough to tell him about her work. "I'm hardly a weakling. I wouldn't have lasted a day in emergency care if I was."

"Holly." Brooks took hold of her hand. "I'm not criticizing you, okay? I'm just sorry you ran into this guy today." His jawline tensed and his eyes narrowed, turning his face into a dangerous mask. "I'd like to inflict a little pain on him in return."

"He was out of his head."

"He chose to get that way."

"I know, but..." She broke off, shaking her head. "What happened today just goes with my job."

"I know." Brooks's fingers tightened around hers. She looked directly into his eyes. "I do know, Holly."

He did, she realized. Unlike Joel, who had never understood why she would choose the emergency room over working in some nice, safe doctor's office, Brooks knew exactly why she could go through days like this one and return to work on Monday. Because, like her, Brooks was committed to work that could change from dull to dangerous in a heartbeat. Else he wouldn't be a cop.

And she'd sworn not to fall for a cop. She had learned her lesson about cops before Zane was born.

With that decade-old promise beating like a drum in her head, Holly pulled her hand from Brooks's. She managed a weak but hopefully impersonal smile. "Goodness. I didn't intend to talk shop. Joel hates it when I talk about the hospital. It's so grim, he says."

Brooks studied her with an inscrutable expression. "Does Joel talk about his work?"

"Not much."

"Lucky you."

"It's not that I don't want to hear about what he does," she said hastily. "Joel is very successful. He has many wealthy, influential clients. He's constantly around interesting people—"

"I'm sure." A grin crooked Brooks's lips. "So why did you break up with him?"

Startled, Holly stared at him. "What?"

"Since Joel is so successful and you've made it abundantly clear that success is what you're looking for in a man, I was just wondering why you told him you didn't want to see him again."

"Who told you that? Nana?" Angry heat flew to Holly's cheeks. "I knew I shouldn't have—"

"It was Zane."

That shocked her into silence. She hadn't broken off with Joel until Wednesday evening, and since then, there'd been little chance for a serious talk with her son. She'd been planning to tell him tonight before she came home and found him with Brooks.

"I didn't know Zane knew," she said finally.

"He told me he listened at the top of the staircase when you and Joel talked the other night. I guess maybe you and the accountant's conversation got a little heated."

Her anger returned. Ignoring the complaints of sore muscles, she quickly rose and sped upstairs, half-expecting to find a little boy with his face pressed close to the banisters, listening to her and Brooks. Instead, she found Zane in bed, with lights out and eyes closed, looking the picture of angelic innocence. If he were feigning sleep, he was doing a very good job. She decided to take up the subject of eavesdropping with him in the morning.

Brooks was waiting for her at the bottom of the stairs. "Everything okay?"

"Until I get hold of him tomorrow."

Grinning, he held out her coffee mug. "You look like you could use another of these. So could I."

She led the way down the hallway to the kitchen and shook her head as she poured coffee for both of them. From a cabinet, she took out a bottle of brandy, un-opened since a friend had presented it to Nana last Christmas. "Care for some of this in your coffee?"

"Sure. Just a bit, though."

She poured half a shot in each of their mugs, then took a long sip of the spirit-enriched brew. "What did Zane tell you about me and Joel?" she asked Brooks finally.

He took a seat at the kitchen table and made him-self at home by propping his feet in the cane-bottomed chair beside him. "This is a nice room, too. Want to tell me all about decorating it?"

"Brooks," Holly said in warning. "What did Zane say?"

"I don't think you want to hear this."

"Darn." She sat down at the end chair nearest him. "I am his mother. Tell me."

"It was pretty garbled. All Zane was sure of was that Joel thought you'd change your mind if you slept with him."

Groaning, Holly propped her elbow on the table and dropped her chin in her palm. "Go on."

"Zane doesn't seem to be too sure what 'sleeping together' entails."

She was surprised. "I can assure you he knows about sex."

Brooks chuckled before taking another sip of cof-fee. "Oh, I'll bet he knows more than you think."

"Then how come he didn't know what Joel was getting at?"

"Joel said 'sleeping with,' not 'making love' or 'having sex' or—"

Holly held up a hand to stop him. "All right, all right. I know all the euphemisms, but maybe Zane doesn't. And maybe he was just putting you on about what he knows. But what I want to know is what you said when my son told you all this."

"I didn't give him any detailed explanations about what dumb old Joel wanted, if that's what you're asking."

"Good."

"I just agreed with him that you had come to your senses and decided Joel was too dull to bother with." Brooks leaned forward. "That is what you decided, isn't it, Holly? That Joel is much too boring?"

She looked down at her coffee, took a deep breath, then centered her gaze on Brooks. "Yeah," she whispered. "That's what I decided."

"Then why are you still bringing him up, hiding behind a relationship that's over?"

"Why do you care?"

He swung his legs out of the chair beside him and turned to face her. Slowly, almost reluctantly, it seemed to her, he touched her cheek, curling his fingers so that the tips just skimmed her jaw. His eyes were very blue, very serious, as he said, "I think you know why I'm interested."

"Because you think I might sleep with you?"

"Would you?"

His low, intimate invitation sent Holly's heartbeat racing. She wondered for a moment what she would do if she were someone else, a woman who hadn't learned the consequences of passion the hard way.

Brooks obviously hoped she was a less wise woman. He leaned closer, so close she could appreciate the spiky fan of dark lashes around his eyes and catch the soap-and-water-clean scent of his skin. "Would you, Holly? Tell me you would."

He was good at seduction. Too good, she thought. That made her more angry than excited, but she kept her aggravation in check, deciding instead to give Brooks Casey some of his own medicine.

"Before I tell you if I would or not, let me ask you a few questions." Bending her head close to his, she lifted a hand to brush a wave of his dark hair off his forehead. She kept her voice low, her gaze on his. "What would you do... if I kissed you?"

Not waiting for a response, she followed through on the promise, intending just to give him a taste. Once their mouths met, though, it was harder than she had planned to break away. He kissed so well, opening his lips so easily, sliding his tongue over hers with such smooth, arousing skill. But she managed to pull back, still intent on torturing him.

"And what if I did this?" she said, getting up and settling herself on the hard muscles of his powerful thighs.

"I'd like that very much," Brooks replied teasingly. With a strong but gentle grip, he threaded his fingers through the hair at the nape of her neck and brought her lips back down to his. His other hand lifted to her shoulder, pulling her close. Once more, he kissed her in that devouring, all-consuming way.

Head spinning, Holly tried to resist. When she struggled, he broke the kiss, though he still held her on his lap.

"Am I hurting your arms?" he murmured close against her mouth.

"No, but—"

"I wouldn't hurt you," he continued as he stroked tender fingers down her bruised right arm. "I'd never hurt you, Holly."

"Brooks—"

Taking her chin in his hand, he cut short her protest by kissing her again.

She gave up all pretense at resistance, giving herself over to the moment, to his touch as he slipped a hand down her legging-encased thigh, to his voice as he crooned low, sweet words in between kisses, to the knowledge that the flesh growing rigid beneath her bottom was clear evidence of the effect this was having on him. She realized dimly that they could be naked, or naked enough, in a matter of seconds. That she could straddle his hips, rock with him to heaven in this chair. They both could have what they were craving—a few moments of mind-blowing release. She was tempted. Dear Lord, it had been so very long since she had felt this way, and she was so very tempted.

Only when Brooks's palm cupped her breast was she jarred back to reality. "Don't." She caught his hand and pulled it away from the breast that had puckered so readily beneath his touch.

As before, he backed off without a protest other than the groan elicited from deep in his throat. Though he wasn't kissing her, or touching her where she didn't want to be touched, he still held her tight.

She could feel him breathing deeply as he buried his face against her shoulder.

"I'm feeling a little sympathy for Joel," he muttered after a few moments had passed.

"I'm sorry. I didn't intend things to get so...so heavy."

His chuckle rumbled in his chest. "Yes, you could say it got...*heavy.*"

Because she knew, *felt,* exactly what he was referring to, Holly murmured another apology and slipped off his lap.

He caught her hand before she could move too far away. "Why stop?" he said, drawing her palm to his lips. "Was I just moving too fast?"

"No, it's just me." Feeling guilty for having started this little escapade, she pulled her hand away. "I just don't do these things, Brooks."

"Ever?"

She picked up their coffee mugs and walked to the sink instead of answering him. But he followed and turned her around to face him, repeating, "Not ever?"

"Never."

He blew out a frustrated breath. "And I thought Joel was just a clumsy clod."

That made her aggravation return. "While you are so very, very slick, of course."

"What's that supposed to mean?"

"Just that you've probably been planning on this happening."

"Not hardly."

She ignored his dry reply. "I bet you do this kind of thing regularly."

"You mean sex?"

"I mean seduction. Wham-bam, thank you, ma'am. A tumble in the sheets or on the kitchen table. Whatever's handy. I'm sure you find new places and new conquests all the time."

Staring in amazement at her lovely, angry face, Brooks thought of all the nights he had spent alone since his past relationship went sour. He thought of the sure thing he had passed up with Julie tonight. He thought of all the times in the last few months when the opportunity for a fast and furious tumble had presented itself. He didn't flatter himself into thinking he was some sort of heartthrob, but there had been chances. At a party this September. With a girl he met in a bar. With that teacher his sister had fixed him up with a few weeks back. He realized that none of that hello-goodbye stuff had appealed to him lately, even before he'd run into this particular woman.

But he wasn't telling Holly any of that. And he wasn't going to be angry at her because she had put on the brakes between them tonight. She was using her head, while another part of the anatomy had been guiding his actions.

Accordingly, he backed away from her. "I honestly didn't come here to seduce you, Holly."

She sagged against the counter, like a sail left without a breeze. "I know. I'm the one who kissed you."

"But I certainly didn't do any protesting. I was completely willing."

Sighing, she shoved a hand through the tumbled waves of her auburn page boy. "I guess I'm feeling a little confused these days."

"Because of breaking up with Joel."

"Because of you."

That straightforward admission took him by surprise. It was his turn to lean against the counter before darting a quick look at her troubled face. "What's happening here, Holly?"

She stepped in front of him. "I'm not sure."

Without pausing to think, he touched her cheek again. "Monday night, after I kissed you, I kept telling myself to back away, to let this go. I felt like there was something between us. Something big. But I figured you'd be mad at me."

"Why?"

"Because I kissed you like that and then walked away."

"Actually..." A smile played across her lips. "That intrigued me."

"But I didn't know that," he said. "All I knew was that you were a woman who said she wasn't interested in me, who was dating a guy who drives a car that costs almost as much as my house." He paused, watching her face closely. "And I knew I was a guy not interested in commitment."

A shadow crossed her features. "So you stayed away."

"I figured it was best, that you wouldn't even want me to talk to Zane. But then, today, when he called, I finally gave in, decided to see what—"

Holly, blinking, held up a hand to stop him. "Wait a minute. Back up. You said Zane called you."

"This afternoon."

"I thought *you* called him."

"No, he called. He invited me to dinner. He told me you knew..." The words trailed away as her expression changed. Now that he thought back on it, he didn't actually remember Zane's saying she knew. The little scamp had tricked him into coming over here. He was smart enough to realize Brooks probably wouldn't come if Holly didn't know. "But you didn't know, did you?"

"No."

Brooks could tell she was upset about this, though he wasn't sure why. "It doesn't matter, Holly. I had told you I was going to call him and set up a time to have a little chat. I was glad to hear from him, actually."

"But you hadn't planned on calling before he did."

He shifted from foot to foot, wondering why her voice was so cold all of a sudden. "No," he told her. "I didn't plan to call."

"Not Zane or me."

Never in Brooks's life had he wanted to lie so much. He wanted to say he had been reaching for the phone when Zane's call came through. But that wasn't true. The truth was, he had been in full-scale retreat from her and her son, from the cozy domesticity of this house, from becoming involved with someone like her. That was the way it was. And she knew it. He saw it in her face.

He caught her hand as she turned away. "Holly, it doesn't matter. Just because I didn't call doesn't mean I was lying a minute ago. It doesn't mean I was expecting to get lucky. I can assure you I expected anything but that from you. You don't operate that way."

"I don't operate at all," she snapped. "I'm just this single mother with this meddling kid. And I was foolish enough to feel a little excited because I thought you had called. Nana Flora had me convinced you wanted to see me. And now, I find out you didn't call, at all. It's . . . it's ego deflating."

Brooks couldn't stop his grin. He took her other hand, pulled her toward him. "I'm sure I could think of something to repair any damage to your ego, Miss MacPherson."

She hung back. "Brooks, this isn't a good idea. Even if we've admitted being wildly attracted to each other—"

"Wildly?" he repeated, still smiling. "Are you wild for me, Holly?"

"Stop that," she said, though the corners of her mouth were twitching. "No matter what's going on here between us, we're still the same people we were when we met. We still want very different things. We've both been clear about that."

"But couldn't we forget?" he cajoled. "For about . . . oh, a half hour? Forty-five minutes?"

"Brooks," she murmured, clearly weakening. "Come on, now, let's think—"

The shriek of his pager cut off whatever she was going to say. Muttering about bad timing, Brooks unclipped it from his belt and pressed a button to see who was calling. Work, of course.

"Stay just as you are," he told Holly before crossing the kitchen to pick up the telephone receiver. "This is probably nothing. That's all it's been at work all this week. One big nothing."

But Holly could see from the rapid change in his expression that this was definitely something. Brooks listened, barked a few short words into the receiver, hung up and then stood, hand over his mouth, looking down at the floor.

"Brooks?" She went to his side. "What is it?"

He glanced up, his lips pursed, much different than the man who had been teasing her only moments ago. "It's my partner," he said.

"What?"

"They found him down by the river."

Holly sucked in her breath. "Not dead."

"Not yet, anyway. He's at your hospital. I've got to get over there."

"I could go—"

"No." That short word rang with finality as Brooks pushed through the door and into the foyer.

"But, Brooks," Holly said, following him. "I'd like to go."

He grabbed his coat off the stand beside the stairs and opened the front door. "Stay here, Holly."

She trailed him onto the porch. "You're upset, Brooks. Please don't go alone."

On the bottom step, he turned to face her. "I don't want you to come."

That sent her back a step, but Brooks made no apologies. He gave her only one last, bleak look before he raced to his car. He left in a screech of tires, a blue light flashing on the dash of his car.

In the cool night air, Holly stood alone, watching him go.

Chapter Five

By seven o'clock Saturday morning, the doctors said Markowitz would make it. Since his jaw was broken and wired shut, however, he couldn't tell anyone exactly what had happened to him. But even the most inept of detectives could have pieced together the story. It was Captain Dixon who spelled things out to Brooks, who had been joined by Mike and Donna at the hospital early on Saturday.

"Markowitz got a tip, followed it and got ambushed."

"But why beat up the kid?" Mike asked.

"He was chosen as a messenger." First looking up and down the hospital corridor, Dixon stepped closer to his officers and lowered his voice. "There was a note found pinned to Markowitz's coat. It says, 'I'm back, Casey. D.W.'"

"Dante Wilson." Donna sucked in her breath and looked at Brooks.

If possible, he felt even more numb than last night when he had arrived here to find Markowitz in a near coma, his face beaten till he was barely recognizable. Emergency surgery had repaired a punctured lung and a splintered thigh bone. All through the night, Brooks had sat on one side of Markowitz's wife while Dixon sat on the other. It was only the second time Brooks had met his partner's spouse, but both times they had been brought together at this hospital. Unlike the first occasion, however, Brooks didn't crack a smile. He simply sat in silence until the doctor came to tell them Markowitz—Dan—was out of the woods. There was some question, unfortunately, about whether Markowitz's leg would ever be quite the same. And they might have to do plastic surgery on his face. They wouldn't know until after the swelling went down.

As he absorbed the physician's information, Brooks had waited, thinking at any moment Dan's devastated young wife was going to turn to him, tell him it was all his fault, rail at him as he was railing at himself inside. But she didn't. She kept her cool while Brooks boiled in his own anger and guilt.

"I know what you're thinking," Dixon told him now, as the news about Dante's note sunk in.

"This is my fault. Dante wants me."

Dixon brushed aside that possibility. "If revenge were all he were after, you know he would have ordered a hit long ago. You'd have already been popped."

Brooks knew that was true. If his life were truly in danger, there had been ample opportunity to take him down before this. There was no reason to beat up Markowitz. Dante, wily fox that he was, was just playing games with them, the same as usual.

Mike broke in, "You can't blame yourself for this, Brooks. Markowitz knew better than to go out alone."

"We argued yesterday."

"So what?" Donna said. "DeWitt and I argue almost every day. But I still would have called him before going out alone to check out a lead, especially when there'd been no leads at all for a week."

"But you two are partners. You're in sync. Me and Markowitz—"

"Are getting there," Dixon said. "Just getting there, Casey."

"Besides," Mike added, "even when you had no partner, you had the instincts to smell a setup, Brooks. If you had gotten this tip, you would have called us or some uniforms. You wouldn't have gone in blind. And Markowitz shouldn't have, either. He may be young, but he isn't stupid."

But Brooks shook off their concerns, remaining silent until the two other detectives left. When they were out of hearing range, Brooks turned to Dixon. "You know Dante has to pay for this."

His captain scowled. "Don't be a cowboy. This isn't the wild West, and you can't challenge Dante to a shoot-out for revenge. I think we should pull back, remain watchful and let Dante show himself. If the man is truly trying to reassert himself in the drug trafficking in this town, we'll know it soon."

Brooks stared at him in shock. "You mean you're just going to let what happened to Markowitz go unanswered?"

"Of course not!"

A passing nurse shushed Dixon, and he pulled Brooks over to the side of the corridor, getting right in his face. "We've got nothing here, Casey. No witnesses. No fingerprints on the note. Nothing but the initials 'D.W.'"

"But everyone knows—"

"Screw that. You know we've got to have something concrete. And all we've got right now is the iffy sighting a week ago of a drug lord who supposedly retired to the Bahamas two years ago."

"And the dealer who said Dante was back?"

"Made bail and has disappeared," Dixon muttered.

"Great, just great."

Dixon grunted his agreement. "But beyond that, my best detectives, including you, have spent the entire week looking for Dante, for anyone who will even say they've seen him. But even if he is seen, no one can prove he's done anything wrong. We've got nothing on him. We've never had anything we could pin directly on Dante. So right now, I say we back off. He'll come to us."

"You know that's not my style."

"But you're not the boss." Dixon shook one long finger at Brooks for emphasis. "So go home."

He did as he was told. He resisted the urge to start combing the scum pits of the city in search of Dante. Instead, he caught some sleep, then went back to the hospital that evening. A check with the guard stationed at Markowitz's door told him his partner had awakened. Swallowing hard, Brooks went in.

As he neared the bed, the young officer's eyes fluttered open. At least, Brooks thought they opened. His face was so swollen it was hard to tell. What was easier to notice was the way his fingers moved at his side. With cautious movements, Brooks put out his hand and covered the wiggling fingers with his own. For a few minutes, he just stood that way, his gut twisting.

"I'm sorry," he whispered finally. "I'm going to be sorry for this for a long, long time. But somehow, we're going to make Dante sorrier."

Markowitz's fingers moved under his again. Brooks couldn't tell if that was confirmation or condemnation or muscle spasms. But he didn't need a reply. He just hoped the young officer could hear him.

He stayed by Markowitz's side for several minutes, until he seemed to be sleeping. Then Brooks stepped outside and found Holly in the corridor, leaning against the wall across from Markowitz's door.

"He wouldn't let me in," she said, nodding at the guard. "I wanted to check on your partner."

"He pulled through."

"They told me that downstairs. I got called in to work tonight. There's a flu bug going around, and they're shorthanded. I'm on a break now."

Brooks led her a few steps down the corridor, away from the guard. He wished Holly hadn't come up here. He didn't want to look at her, didn't want to think about last night. When he'd been kissing her, some punk had been pummeling his partner's head. Turning from her concerned gaze, he glanced down the hall and saw Markowitz's wife standing in front of the nurse's station. He squeezed his eyes shut, not wanting to see her, either.

"Are you okay?" Holly asked, taking hold of his arm.

"Yeah, just peachy."

She drew back. "You seem angry."

"How am I supposed to seem when someone almost beat my partner to death?"

"Is that what happened? The newspaper said—"

"—only what the department wants them to say. You're not going to get the truth from the newspaper." He shook his head in disgust. "You might have been raised by a policeman, but you don't know the score, do you?"

"Why don't you tell me the score? Tell me what happened."

He started to speak, then broke off. "Listen, Holly, I appreciate your concern, but I don't want to talk about this."

Her worried, dark-eyed gaze swept over him. "I think you need to talk. Let's go sit down somewhere."

"No." Looking up, Brooks saw Markowitz's wife was walking down the hall. He couldn't face her right now. And he didn't want to be with Holly, either. He didn't want her comfort or her sweetness or the sanctuary he would no doubt find in her arms. He knew it would become all too easy to rely on her. If he wasn't careful, the two of them could become hopelessly entangled. And that was no good. Because if that happened, then sooner or later Holly could end up just like the young Mrs. Markowitz, sitting through a night of hell, waiting to see if Brooks lived or died.

"I'm sorry, Holly. I've got to get out of here." He stalked off.

For the second night in a row, Holly stood staring after him.

"Excuse me. Nurse?"

She turned to face a plump young blonde with red-rimmed eyes and a panicked look on her face. "I saw you talking to that man," the woman said, nodding toward Brooks's fast-disappearing back. "Is there something wrong? Is my husband okay?"

"Your husband?" Holly frowned in confusion until realization hit. "You must be married to the policeman who was brought in last night."

"Yes, and that was his partner. Is there something—"

"There's nothing wrong," Holly soothed, patting the woman's arm. "I'm a friend of Lieutenant Casey's."

The younger woman rocked back on her heels, letting out a sigh of relief. "Thank goodness. When I saw the two of you talking and watched him take off like that, I was afraid..." She put a trembling hand to her mouth. "I was just so afraid."

"As far as I know, your husband is doing fine. Brooks and I..." Holly stopped, shaking her head. "Brooks and I were just talking. He's very upset about what happened."

"He blames himself, I think. Because he wasn't with Dan last night."

"Oh." Holly was beginning to understand why Brooks looked like a man in serious pain. "He was with me when the call came in."

The woman introduced herself as Kendra Markowitz. "So you and Lieutenant Casey are friends?"

"I guess you could say that," Holly said wryly.

For the first time, Kendra managed a smile. "Something tells me it would be easy not to be sure of things around Lieutenant Casey. He can be pretty intimidating, from what Dan tells me."

"That's an understatement."

"He was good to me last night, though. He was right there, all night. I really appreciated it, even though I don't even think I told him so."

"I think there might be a decent guy buried under all that tough-as-nails bravura."

Kendra nodded. "What is it about cops? They put on their badges and their guns and they think they can't show what they're feeling. They think that's weak." She brushed her hair back from her forehead, looking suddenly exhausted. "It's a wonder they get married at all, much less stay that way."

Holly wasn't surprised by the statement. She knew it from firsthand experience, from observing her grandparents and from trying to forge a bond with the young officer who had fathered Zane. And yet here she was, against her better judgment, all torn up inside over another cop. A big, mixed-up detective who wasn't looking for what she wanted to give. This was just what she had always sworn not to do.

After excusing herself from Kendra, Holly hurried to the nurse's lounge. In the bathroom, she leaned over the sink and splashed cold water on her face. She felt hot and cold and sick all over. And it wasn't the flu. It was from knowing how much worse she was going to feel when Brooks didn't call her, when she never heard from him again.

After last night, even after the way he had left, she had been filled with this stupid exuberance. She had felt so happy she wanted to sing. All because of a little kissing, a little touching, a little teasing. What a fool she was. "A born-again fool," she muttered to her reflection in the mirror.

She was drying her face when her name was called over the loudspeaker. A glance at her watch revealed her break had been over for some time. Holly sped through the halls and down to emergency, where a woman in imminent danger of delivering a child claimed her immediate attention.

This was important, she told herself. This mattered, not some foolish feelings for a policeman she barely knew who worked overtime sealing himself off from the world.

Unfortunately, that buoying knowledge didn't lift her spirits through the next week.

It was Thanksgiving week, normally one of Holly's favorite times of the year. She loved the scents of spices from Nana Flora's baking in the kitchen. She loved the quickening pace of the city as it geared up for the holiday season. She loved the leaves that rained down in colorful bands in the yard. Here on the Mississippi Delta, the fall foliage was still lush, even near the end of November. And though the nights were crisp, the days were often warm and were always lit by a special hue of golden sunshine.

This year was no less beautiful than any other Thanksgiving in the past. As usual, Holly, Zane and Nana Flora had Charleen and Bob and their two boys from next door over for the big meal. They all stuffed themselves, watched football and played board games. Holly had even wangled Friday off from work. She and Zane braved the holiday crowds at the mall and made a dent in their Christmas shopping.

Her son mentioned Brooks several times, but Holly explained what had happened to Brooks's partner. She cautioned Zane not to expect to see Brooks any time soon, because he was sure to be busy looking for whoever had hurt Markowitz.

Of course, news that Brooks was tracking down a bad guy had made him even more intriguing to Zane. Holly knew the boy would be hurt when Brooks didn't come around again. But she also knew Zane would get over it. Some other obsession would arrive to claim his youthful enthusiasm.

But what about her?

Holly avoided examining her feelings about Brooks. She told herself she had no business worrying about a man she barely knew, one who had never even taken her out on a date. She threw herself into activities, attending the theater with Nana Flora, the movies with Charleen, church on Sunday morning. That afternoon, she and Zane and Marcus raked leaves, spending almost as much time jumping into the colorful heaps as they did gathering them up. It was a wonderful day, the perfect end to a pleasant holiday weekend.

And yet, that night, as she sat in the window seat of her room, Holly cried. Not because Brooks hadn't called—Holly hadn't cried over a man since Zane's father left her. And even before that, she had never wasted much energy or time on tears. Nana Flora and Papa Jake had always said tears were a last resort. But tonight, they seemed right. Holly felt lonely. And alone.

Zane found her crying. She thought he was asleep, so she sat up, startled when he materialized in the darkness at her side. "What's wrong, Mom?"

Hastily wiping tears away, she just shook her head, not trusting herself to speak. As if he understood, Zane just squeezed in beside her on the seat. Grateful for his presence, for the warmth his very existence brought her, she leaned her head against his. She was glad of the darkness, however, for tears continued to slide silently down her cheeks.

"Did I do something?" Zane asked after several moments had passed.

"Of course not," she choked out, slipping her arm around him. Why was it, she wondered, that even the most secure of children always worried that they were at the root of all problems? "I'm just feeling sad tonight. No reason. Just sad."

"Did you miss Papa Jake this weekend? I remember Nana Flora cried last Thanksgiving and said it was because Papa Jake wasn't here."

Forcing herself to get a grip on her runaway emotions, Holly nodded. "Maybe that's it. Maybe it's just not having him here with us that's made me sad and lonely."

"You're lonely?" The youngster turned to her, the moonlight revealing the look of surprise on his face. "But I'm here."

She managed a chuckle. "Yes, you are. And I'm so glad. But before you came in here, I was feeling all alone. Maybe that's why you got out of bed, because you knew I needed a cuddle from my favorite guy."

"I got up because I had to go to the bathroom," he said dryly. "I heard you crying on the way back."

Holly laughed again, more easily this time. "Well, for whatever reason, I'm glad you came in. I'm feeling a lot better."

"You sure?"

"Sure, I'm sure." Leaning down, she touched her forehead to his. "Now, get off to bed again."

Zane was reluctant to do so. Not because he wasn't sleepy. He was really tired after all that leaf raking. But he didn't want to leave his mom alone when she looked so sad. She had laughed and everything and said she was fine, but he knew she wasn't. Her voice sounded funny—all hoarse and scratchy. He couldn't remember her crying before, except maybe when Papa Jake died. And maybe the time Zane fell out of his tree house and she thought he was dead, but all that was really the matter was he'd had the wind knocked out of his lungs. She had cried after she knew he was breathing, but those were a happy kind of tears, all mixed up with laughter. Tonight, there was nothing happy about her.

In the end, he went back to bed because she said he had to. But tired as he was, he couldn't sleep. He kept thinking about her being lonely. He wondered what Brooks was doing tonight, if he might be alone, too. He wanted to call him. But Zane understood when his mother said he shouldn't bother Brooks for a while. Brooks's friend had been hurt.

As a Knight of the Woodmere Realm, Zane knew how important it was to take care of your friends. But wasn't his mother Brooks's friend, too? Brooks had said so, that night he came for dinner. He said even though there wasn't much chance of his becoming Zane's dad, he would be happy to be a friend to all of them—Zane, Nana and his mom. So maybe if he knew how much Mom needed him, he would come if Zane called.

Zane closed his eyes, thinking about what they had talked about at the Knights club meeting this week, about not giving up on your quest. Mr. Robinson said you had to keep trying, even when it looked like you might fail. But Zane had almost given up. He'd let Brooks convince him that being a friend to them was almost as good as being a father. And that wasn't true. Zane was sure his mom wouldn't be feeling lonely tonight, wouldn't be crying, if Brooks were married to her. But what could Zane do about it?

He thought he had run out tricks for getting them together. He didn't think Brooks would fall for the dinner invitation again. He didn't think his mother would like it much, either. But there had to be something....

The next day, on the playground at school, Zane gathered his buddies around him. He had intended to keep his quest a secret from everyone but Marcus and maybe his nana. But he required more brainpower to make this work. So first, he laid out the situation and what he wanted to accomplish. Then he issued the challenge, "Okay, guys. I need a plan. I need everybody to think. Think really, really hard...."

Pausing just outside the doors to the elementary school gymnasium, Brooks straightened his tie and took a moment to wipe parking-lot dust from his highly polished shoes. It had been a while since he had worn his blues, as they called their uniforms, but since Zane had invited him to speak at "What I Want to Be when I Grow up Day," Brooks wanted to look the part of a policeman.

He couldn't quite believe he was here, after having sworn to stay away from the MacPhersons. It was Donna's fault. She had been in the office when Zane called yesterday and Brooks cut him off with intentional rudeness. Maybe he had been gruffer to the boy than he should have been. But when he hung up the phone, Donna had demanded to know if it was Holly's son he had been talking to. Brooks didn't even remember telling the female detective Holly or Zane's names. But she knew them. The same way the woman seemed to know and see things all the time that Brooks didn't remember telling her. She called it having a good memory and great intuition. He and Mike called it plain spooky.

Whatever the case, Donna had read Brooks the riot act about being mean to a little kid. "Maybe you enjoy walking around here all sulled up like a bullfrog," she said with her dark eyes snapping. "You're so busy kicking yourself for Markowitz getting hurt that you can't see anything else that's going on. Most of us can take your ill humor. We're used to seeing it from time to time. But do you have to take it out on a little boy who happens to like you?"

"He doesn't just like me," Brooks retorted. "He wants me to be his father. And I'm no one's father. I'm not father material."

Donna slammed a desk drawer closed and glared at him. "Yeah, yeah, yeah. I know the routine. You're a lone wolf, a singular kind of guy. You got enough togetherness when you were growing up. Well, from where I sit, being alone hasn't done you much good lately.'' With that, she stalked out of the room.

Brooks sat at his desk, feeling like the scum at the bottom of a well bucket. When that was over, however, he called Zane back. That boy, God love him, was as friendly as he'd been before Brooks hung up on him. Brooks didn't know where the little man got his resilience, but he admired him for it. And there was no way he could turn down the invitation to come to Zane's after-school program today. Especially since Brooks planned to use his talk as a way of bringing himself down to size in Zane's eyes. Brooks was uncomfortable with the hero-worship. He wanted Zane and the rest of these boys to see policemen as what they were—just men and women trying to do a job.

Pulling open the gym doors, he walked toward the young boys and adults clustered at the other side of the gym. Zane came running out to meet him, then led him to the group leader. The young, bespectacled fellow thanked Brooks for coming and introduced him to the three other adults who were participating in the day's program. The adults lined up in chairs, and the boys settled in the bleachers. The first parent, a doctor, had begun to talk about what he did when the door slammed at the end of the gym.

And Holly walked in.

A ripple of excitement ran through the assembled boys. And as good as Holly looked in her trim green suit, Brooks didn't think it was her looks that caused the commotion. There was something going on here. Something that could be traced directly to the nine-year-old with the sparkling dark eyes who was squirming in the front row. Brooks gave Zane a stern look before turning back to Holly.

It didn't matter that she was here, he told himself. She meant nothing to him. She was just Zane's mother. A casual acquaintance. Nothing more.

Holly appeared to hesitate when her gaze met Brooks's, but she lifted her chin a notch and kept walking. "Am I late?" she asked the group leader. "Zane told me to be here at three forty-five, and I thought I was early."

"It's no problem," the leader said. "We're just getting started."

She took a seat in the only empty chair, which, of course, just happened to be next to Brooks. From the grins a couple of the boys exchanged, Brooks figured that had been a setup, too.

But that was okay. He could handle it. He didn't look at her once, but he was aware of her every sigh, of every time she folded her hands in her lap or crossed and recrossed her slender legs. He let himself get so rattled that the leader had to say his name twice before Brooks stood to give his presentation to the group.

He got that right, however. In straightforward, direct terms, he let them know that being a policeman wasn't the cop-and-robber deal it looked like on television or at the movies. He explained the boring stuff, the paperwork, the hours of riding around in a car. Then he told them about the danger, illustrating that point with what had happened to Markowitz. The young, eager faces grew serious as he detailed his partner's injuries. Brooks could see that he got through to his audience.

In closing, he said, "Some of you probably think being a cop is sort of like being a hero on the TV shows you like to watch. Well, I won't lie, sometimes it feels that way. But a good policeman is just a man or a woman who wants to do the right thing, who wants to take care of people who need help. Like these other jobs you've heard about here today, police work is a big responsibility. You may think my saying this is kind of corny, but when cops do their jobs well, they know they've made a difference in other people's lives. And in my opinion, that's more important than making a lot of money or chasing bad guys or being anyone's hero."

In the front row, Zane sat up a little straighter, grinning at Brooks with pride as he led the others in applause. To his surprise, Brooks found himself beaming at the boy. He didn't know why, but Zane did something to him. From the minute they'd met, the kid had been so open and accepting and warm. He touched Brooks in a special way, a way that no one other than his family had. It was strange, but pretty darn pleasant.

Still smiling, Brooks turned to sit down and looked Holly straight in the face for the first time since she had walked in. Her eyes were wide and dark and shining as brightly, as proudly as Zane's. That expression, that straight-from-her-heart approval washed over him like a tidal wave of warmth. He didn't hesitate when she put out her hand. He took it and held on, squeezing her fingers lightly while the group's leader made her introduction.

She stood and talked to the boys, but Brooks had no idea what she said. He was lost in the sound of her voice. And he was wondering why even his best intentions were derailed when it came to her. He knew his mother would say that maybe his intentions weren't on the right track.

Somehow, he made it through the question-and-answer session that followed their presentations. Zane ran up as soon as they were dismissed, chattering excitedly. His leader thanked them, other boys came up to say hello, other parents tried to chat, as well. But Brooks and Holly didn't pay much attention. They were too busy looking at each other.

Miraculously, they made their way out of the gym. Zane was prancing in front of them, waving his aluminum-foil-covered paper sword in the air, babbling on about being a cop when he grew up.

Brooks heard little except Holly's quiet "How've you been?"

"Not good." He took her hand, threaded his fingers through hers and decided to speak his mind, no matter how foolish that might be. "I'm feeling much better now."

"Are you?"

"Much, much better." He smiled and was ridiculously elated when she grinned back.

"I'm really glad. I was worried about you."

"I acted like a jackass the last time we talked."

"You were worried about your partner, blaming yourself."

He frowned. "How do you know that?"

"I figured it out."

"You and Donna," he muttered, shaking his head. "You're spooky."

"Who's Donna?"

He told her about Mike and Donna, adding, "I think you'd probably like them."

"Maybe I'll meet them sometime."

"Maybe," he echoed as they stopped beside her car. He took her other hand because he couldn't stand the thought of releasing her. Perhaps she felt the same way, because she didn't protest, didn't make any move to get in her car. Brooks figured they looked like goofy junior-high-school lovebirds, standing here, grinning at each other in the late-November afternoon sunshine. But they might have just stayed there if it weren't for Zane.

"I'm starving," the boy announced. "Can't we go for pizza?"

"Sounds good to me," Brooks agreed.

Holly agreed. "Nana Flora's going out with a friend from church tonight."

"Then let's go."

They let Zane choose the place where they should meet, and of course, he picked the noisiest pizza parlor in town, the one filled with other kids and video games. It was hardly romantic, but maybe that was for the best, Brooks decided. Zane took off to feed quarters into his favorite games and left Brooks and Holly alone in a corner booth where they sat next to each other, picked at their pizza and devoured each other with their eyes. If it had been some quiet, dim spot, instead of a roomful of rowdy youngsters and their parents, Brooks wasn't sure what they might have ended up doing.

The pull between them was almost frightening in its intensity. Brooks knew he had been in deep lust before, but that was nothing like what he was experienc-

ing with Holly tonight. The attraction had a mind of
its own, he decided. It had taken them over like some
weird extraterrestrial growth from one of the outer-
space TV movies he and his brothers and sisters had
watched late on Saturday nights when they were kids.

Holly echoed his thoughts. "Do you feel like you're
in an episode from the 'Twilight Zone?'"

"Absolutely."

"I know the plot line." She nodded toward Zane,
who was busy at the controls of a nearby machine.
"He's a real little boy. But you and I, we're just puppets. And he's controlling us, manipulating us, putting us together in places where we didn't plan to be."

"Maybe he's just looking out for us. He wants his
puppets to be happy."

Elbows on the table, she leaned her chin against her
folded hands. "You mean he wants us to feel safe and
secure?"

"Right."

"But I don't feel safe, Brooks." The teasing light
disappeared from her eyes. "I feel like I'm walking a
tightrope over a pit."

"Are there alligators below?"

"There's one. He wears a badge and he chases bad
guys and he's often in danger, and he believes everything he told all those little boys this afternoon. And
part of that is why I like him so much. And part of
that is why he scares me to death."

Trying to defuse her sudden mood shift, he ran a
finger down her tantalizing little turned-up nose. "You
are a tasty morsel, it's true. That old alligator may
have to gobble you up if you fall."

"I'm not joking," she said unnecessarily.

NO RISK, NO OBLIGATION TO BUY... NOW OR EVER!

CASINO JUBILEE

"Scratch'n Match" Game

Here's how to play:

1. Peel off label from front cover. Place it in the space provided opposite. With a coin carefully scratch away the silver box. This makes you eligible to receive two or more free books, and possibly another gift, depending upon what is revealed beneath the scratch-off area.

2. Send back this card and you'll receive specially selected Silhouette Special Editions, which are yours to keep absolutely free!

3. There's no catch. You're under no obligation to buy anything. We charge nothing for your first shipment. And you don't have to make any minimum number of purchases - not even one!

4. The fact is thousands of readers enjoy receiving books by mail from the Reader Service, at least a month before they're available in the shops. They like the convenience of home delivery, and there is no extra charge for postage and packing.

5. We hope that after receiving your free books you'll want to remain a subscriber. But the choice is yours - to continue or cancel, anytime at all! So why not take up our invitation, with no risk of any kind. You'll be glad you did!

*Prices subject to change without notice.

YOURS FREE!

You'll look like a million dollars when you wear this elegant necklace! It's cobra link chain is a generous 18" long and its lustrous simulated pearl is mounted in an attractive pendant.

(Pictured larger to show d

CASINO JUBILEE
"Scratch'n Match" Game

SCRATCH HERE ?

PLACE LABEL HERE

CHECK CLAIM CHART BELOW
FOR YOUR FREE GIFTS!

4S6SE

YES! I have placed my label from the front cover in the space provided above and scratched away the silver box. Please send me all the gifts for which I qualify. I understand that I am under no obligation to purchase any books, as explained on the back and on the opposite page. I am over 18 years of age.

BLOCK CAPITALS PLEASE

MS/MRS/MISS/MR _____

ADDRESS _____

_____

_____ POSTCODE _____

CASINO JUBILEE CLAIM CHART	
🍒 🍒 🍒	WORTH 4 FREE BOOKS A FREE NECKLACE AND MYSTERY GIFT
🔔 🔔 🔔	WORTH 4 FREE BOOKS
🔔 🔔 🍒	WORTH 3 FREE BOOKS — CLAIM N° 1528

Offer closes 31st October 1996. We reserve the right to refuse an application. *Terms and prices subject to change without notice. Offer not available for current subscribers to this series. One application per household. Offer valid in UK and Ireland only. Overseas readers please write for details. Southern Africa write to IBS Private Bag X3010, Randburg 2125.

You may be mailed with offers from other reputable companies as a result of this application. If you would prefer not to share in this opportunity please tick box. ☐

Silhouette Reader Service

FREEPOST

Croydon
Surrey
CR9 3WZ

NO
STAMP
NEEDED

He fell silent, watching her and struggling to say just the right thing to reassure her. "I'm not sure I can give you what you want, Holly. For the first time in my life, I'm thinking I might want that safety and security you're so fond of. But I just don't know. I wish I could make you some kind of promise right now. But I can't. God, I'm not even sure of what I'm feeling. All I'm certain of is that I looked at you this afternoon and felt as if I'd never be able to forgive myself if I didn't try, just *try* to make something with you."

"Something?"

"A relationship, I guess."

"You guess?"

He sat back, frowning. "Please, Holly. Stop pushing. I can't give more than I just did. Can't we just take this moment by moment?"

"I told you. I'm not good at that."

"Because of Zane's father?"

She made an impatient gesture. "I don't know the psychology of what I feel, Brooks. I never went to a shrink. Maybe I should have. Maybe when Zane's father decided he was too young to give up his freedom for an eighteen-year-old and the baby she was carrying, maybe that did something irreversible to me. Or maybe it started before that, when my father was killed and my mother left. Maybe I'm just all screwed up."

"No, you're not," Brooks interrupted. "If you want to talk psychological messes, just look at me. Here I was—raised in the bosom of this big, terrific family. They're the greatest. Right now, any one of them would put their life on the line for me."

He pointed to his chest for emphasis. "*I* should be the person who wants a nice little family, because I know how good it can be. But instead, I've spent the last twelve years or so running from commitment in any form or fashion. And not just from commitment to a woman. Hell, Holly, I never really even had a partner before Markowitz.''

''How did you get away with that?''

''It was an accident at first. My first assigned partner after I made detective had to take medical leave, so I fumbled through on my own with a little help from Mike and Donna. I proved I could solve cases by myself. And then…'' Blowing out a frustrated breath, he looked away.

''Brooks?'' Holly put her hand on his arm.

He kept his eyes averted, not wanting to see her reaction when he said, ''Then I killed somebody.''

She didn't speak, but her fingers tightened around his forearm. Brooks went on, still not looking at her as he explained Lewis Wilson's death. ''I didn't really think it had affected me,'' he added. ''Not at first, anyway. I just went on, doing my job. Then there were little problems that kept cropping up. I froze one day on a bust. I let too much of the paperwork slide. I messed up an investigation. So my captain assigned me this rookie detective—Markowitz. And I've been doing everything I could to blow him off.''

''That's why you blame yourself for his beating?''

He turned to face her again, nodding.

Holly had always heard eyes were the window to the soul. If that were the case, Brooks had one very tortured soul. By nature and training, she was both a comforter and a healer, but she had never wanted that to be her primary role in a relationship. At least not until now. And right now, what she wanted was to take

Brooks in her arms and make his pain go away. She didn't know if that was possible, but she wanted to try.

Quietly, she said, "I know it doesn't do any good to tell you that wasn't your fault."

His wry, crooked grin made a fleeting appearance. "Nope."

"I can't pretend to even understand your guilt."

"You're smart not to try."

"So I guess all I can say is—" she leaned close, playfully bumping her shoulder against his arm "—I'm here any time you want to talk about it."

He smiled. "Any time? You sure about that?"

"Well . . . since I have to get up every morning by five-thirty, I might not be available from about 11:00 p.m. until then. But any time in between . . . hey, I'm yours."

His arm crept around her shoulders, drawing her close as his voice deepened. "That's a mighty provocative offer, Miss MacPherson. I might take it literally."

Holly turned her head, nuzzled the collar of his uniform. His gold lieutenant bar was cold against her cheek. "Maybe that's the way I mean it," she whispered. "Literally."

He dipped his head forward, touching his mouth to hers in the lightest, sweetest of kisses, then murmured, "I sure as hell wish we weren't here."

"Where would you rather be?"

"I might shock you if I said."

"I'm a nurse, remember. I don't shock easily."

He chuckled. "I could put that to the test."

She cocked her head back and smiled up at him teasingly. "That sounds like fun."

"Holly." Her name was half groan, half sigh before he kissed her again.

Drawing away, she shot an anxious look in Zane's direction and was relieved to see him still absorbed in his game.

"He set this up," Brooks said dryly. "So I doubt he would disapprove."

"But if we sit here and neck with all these kids around, he might get a little embarrassed."

"So maybe we should go home."

"At home, he'll be right under our feet."

"Send him to bed."

"That's a possibility. Of course, then we get to wait around for my grandmother to come home."

Groaning again, Brooks laid his head back against the cushioned seat of the booth. "This could get complicated, couldn't it?"

"I think it already is."

They were smiling into each other's eyes again when his pager went off.

"I can't believe the timing of this thing," Brooks muttered. He checked the number and then slid out of the booth and headed for the pay phone outside the pizza parlor.

Holly crossed her arms on the tabletop and considered the afternoon's rather dizzying turn of events. If someone had told her yesterday she'd be sitting with Brooks and discussing the ways and means of a romantic tryst, she'd have laughed in response. She had a hard time believing it was happening now. Was this really her, flirting with Brooks, kissing him, teasing him with sexual innuendos? Was she one hundred percent sure she wanted this—*thing* as he so unpoetically put it—to happen? If she had any doubts, she knew now was the time to back out, before she got in any deeper.

While Holly was thinking over that possibility, Brooks appeared at the door. He waved at her, but before he could cross the crowded room to their booth, Zane intercepted him. He was probably begging for more quarters, she thought. Whatever it was Zane said, however, it made Brooks laugh. He followed the youngster over to one of the larger games, one where they could play one another. Then neither of them spared Holly another glance.

Grumbling to herself after several minutes passed, she gathered up her purse and their jackets and joined them at the game, which Zane appeared to be winning. She stood quietly to one side while his space fighters destroyed Brooks's mother ship. Amid groans and cheers, the two males finally noticed Holly was waiting.

"Thanks for deserting me," she told Brooks with mock severity.

"Your son issued a challenge. I couldn't refuse."

"I killed him," Zane added with glee. "Now he owes me five bucks."

"What?" Holly demanded. "Since when do you bet on video games?"

Zane cast a mischievous glance toward his partner in crime. "Since Brooks said okay."

She turned to the big man beside her. "We don't place bets for money in the MacPherson household."

"Aw, Mom," Zane whined.

"Oh, come on," Brooks added to his plea. "Can't you let it go just this once? I didn't know the rules, and I did place the bet. It's a gentleman's debt that I have to pay."

She wondered how any red-blooded female could resist with those two pair of pleading gazes focused on her. So she gave in, but she nixed the idea of a rematch. "There's school tomorrow," she told Zane when he protested.

As they headed for the exit, Brooks put a hand on his shoulder. "She's right, little man. And we'll play again."

That brought the boy's head up, and a smile wreathed his face as he looked from his mom to Brooks and back again. "Will we? You're really gonna be around?"

"Yes, I think he is," Holly replied as they stepped onto the sidewalk outside the pizza palace.

"Way cool!" Zane commented before beginning a struggle with his jacket.

Brooks moved forward to untangle the arms for the boy, but in the glow of the flashing neon sign, Holly could see he was smiling at her. "Very cool," he said.

There was a promise, a heat, in his gaze that reached down inside her. Right here, right now, in this most inappropriate of spots, Holly felt arousal sharpen inside her. Arousal as pointed as that engendered earlier by his touch and his kiss. Just looking at Brooks made her knees weak, her mouth dry and her pulse race. And all her doubts and worries felt like so much dust in the wind. The last thing she wanted to do was back down or back away from Brooks Casey.

She took a deep breath and followed her instincts. "Maybe you could come home with us now," she told Brooks.

His eyes widened. "Now?"

She took hold of his hand. "Now.

"But your grandmother—"

"Could be made to understand, I think."

She watched the muscles work in his throat as Brooks swallowed. Once, then again. "Holly," he said at last. "I wish I had known...I mean, I got that page and it's not an emergency else I would have left right away, but they do need me to come, and I said I would."

Holly had to laugh. He looked so comical, so torn between duty and pleasure.

But he didn't get the joke. "What's so funny?"

"Just us," she said, still chuckling. "I mean, here I am with all these doubts and excuses, and you're raring to go. Then I make up my mind, and you're going on a call. It's funny, really, when you think about it."

"I think you're hysterical," Brooks told her, still not laughing.

Standing forgotten between them, Zane said, "I don't see what's so funny, either, Mom."

Brooks tousled his hair. "Don't worry about it, kid. Women aren't meant to be understood."

"Hey," Holly objected. "There's no women-bashing allowed in the MacPherson household, either."

"That wasn't bashing," Brooks corrected. "If I had been allowed to complete my statement—"

"Oh, please do," Holly cut in.

"I would have said that women are not to be understood but are to be appreciated and savored. And the special one is worth waiting for."

The tenderness in his tone would have melted the heart of a woman not halfway in love with him. But Holly was, so she did more than melt. Sighing, she slipped her arm through his and wished her son were back inside, rotting his brain with video games. She supposed Brooks felt the same way. She knew he would have kissed her if Zane hadn't made a gagging noise followed by several boos and hisses.

"Wait a minute," Brooks told the boy. "I thought you wanted me to go out with your mom?"

"Just don't do so much of the kissy-pie stuff in front of me, okay?" Zane swallowed, still trying to act as if he was going to be sick.

"Oh, you." Leaving Brooks, Holly took her son by the arm and started toward her car. "Let's get you home before you have an attack."

Brooks followed them, took her keys and opened the car door, admonished Zane to buckle up, then kissed Holly goodbye. A short kiss, in deference to Zane's presence. But there was potent, sexy promise in the "I'll see you soon, very soon" he whispered before she got in the car and drove away.

Holly believed Brooks, but she didn't know exactly how soon he meant. She was glad, however, that she was still awake at half past eleven when she heard a car turn into her driveway. She knew instinctively that it was Brooks. She flew downstairs before he could knock, and she opened the door without pausing to see if it was really him. Even then she didn't say a word. She just stepped into his arms.

"I couldn't wait," he murmured, lifting her off the ground with the strength of his embrace. He kissed a trail of fire up her neck. "I'm really sorry. I know it's so late and you have to get up so early, and I don't expect anything. I mean, I didn't come here to sleep with you."

She drew back. "No?"

"I just had to see you again tonight. Kiss you just once more—"

Holly trapped his explanations beneath her lips.

Somehow, they made it into the foyer and closed the front door, but they stopped near the staircase, kissing, murmuring mindless words of encouragement and pleasure.

She pushed at his jacket, drawing it down his arms. The leather was cool from the night air, the same as his cheeks. But his mouth was warm, and he moved it in such delicious ways across hers. His jacket fell to the floor unheeded. She wrapped her arms tighter around him while he massaged her back through the thin material of her nightgown. She was perfectly willing for him to go on massaging, touching, arousing.

But instead, he stepped away and placed his hands on either side of her face. "I didn't want to want you like this," he whispered fiercely. "I've never driven to a woman's house late at night just for a kiss. I've never felt like this."

She placed her hands over both of his and drew them tight against her chest. "Are you sure it's just a kiss you want?"

With a groan, he brought her close, pressing his lips to her forehead, holding her. "I want everything you have to give, lady. But I don't want it fast. I don't want to be listening for your grandmother or your son or the alarm clock." His voice deepened, lowered. "I want to kiss every inch of you. A couple of times. Then I want to start over again. And when we're through I want to hold you all night long.''

She shivered, anticipation and arousal tightening her nipples and spreading exquisite moisture between her thighs. Weakness claimed her knees. Glad that his strong arms were holding her up, she managed a very shaky laugh. ''Are you sure we have to wait?''

''Listen to you,'' he murmured. ''Is this the woman who told me 'never' just a week before last?''

''She's changed.''

''This is a change for me, too, you know. This waiting.'' He combed his fingers through her hair. ''But I said it tonight. I told Zane—a special woman is worth waiting for. And when we get the timing right, we're going to make this special.''

Sighing with pleasure, she lifted her mouth to his again.

At the top of the stairs, Zane sat with Wondercat at his side, listening with avid interest to what he could hear from downstairs. It was hard to make out everything, but at long last, things seemed to be going right. He couldn't see much with the lights off, but he knew his mom and Brooks were kissing. A lot. With that going on, there might be an end to his quest very soon.

His mom's laughter, light and happy and young sounding, drifted up the stairs. Smiling, Zane leaned against the banister and yawned. Then he jumped when something touched his shoulder. Looking up, he found Nana Flora standing over him.

''Bed,'' she whispered. ''Now.''

''But they're—''

She shushed him with a finger to her lips, and her touch on his arm was firm as she urged him to his room and back under his covers.

"I just wanted to see what happened," he grumbled around another giant-sized yawn.

"Some things are private."

"But do you think they're really getting together this time?"

Nana didn't reply, but her smile beamed just before she turned out his lamp.

Chapter Six

"Don't forget what Nana told us," Zane said from his perch on the back seat of Brooks's off duty car, a late model Bronco. "We can't get a Christmas tree like last year's."

"I know, I know," Holly retorted. "I have my instructions."

Brooks took his eyes off the Saturday-afternoon Christmas-shopping traffic to glance at her. "What was wrong with last year's tree?"

Zane made a sound of disgust. "It was only ten feet too tall."

His mom sent him a warning glare. "That's a slight exaggeration."

"Oh, yeah? Then how come when Marcus's dad cut it off for us, there were enough branches left to decorate their whole house?"

With a raised eyebrow, Brooks looked at Holly. "Didn't you measure the thing before you brought it home?"

Again Zane spoke first. "She doesn't buy Christmas trees like that. She just sees one she likes and gets it whether it'll fit in the living room or not. After she argues about the price, that is. It doesn't matter how it looks."

"Now, that's not true," Holly denied. "I definitely care how it looks. Last year's tree was this big, beautiful Fraser fir. It was so green and thick—"

"All the ornaments just kind of laid on it," Zane muttered.

Brooks burst out laughing. "Sounds like my coming along today is a lifesaver for the MacPherson family Christmas."

Holly crossed her arms. "I've been buying trees for quite a while. You didn't have to come."

"But aren't you glad I did?"

She scowled at him in mock anger for a minute, then let a smile peak through. "I guess so. You are kind of cute."

"Are you guys going to *sweetie* talk all day?" Zane asked, groaning.

"Hey, bud." Brooks met the boy's gaze in the rearview mirror. "Someday you're going to want to know how to *sweetie* talk. So I'd advise you just to sit back and take notes."

"Yeah, right." The youngster might sound contemptuous, but his eyes were shining with happiness, as they'd been every day for the past week and a half.

A week and a half. How amazing to think only ten days had passed since the Tuesday afternoon Holly had walked across her son's school gymnasium. Ten days since Brooks had realized he couldn't ignore or resist Holly's appeal. Ten days of seeing her every day. Ten days and counting since he'd come back to her house and promised to wait until the time was right for them to make love.

Quite honestly, in terms of frustration levels, the time was well overdue. But in terms of what both of them wanted from the relationship, the waiting was okay. Even though Holly seemed every bit as hot for him as he was for her, Brooks knew making love with him would be a big step for her. So putting things off, building the anticipation, was best for her.

For him, the waiting was a test. To see if he might really make it with a woman like Holly. His romantic past was littered with women who were nothing more than temporary playmates, women who, at this point in a relationship, would no longer hold his interest if he weren't sexually involved with them. Sex had been a very important component of every relationship— failed though they might all be—that he'd had before Holly. But from her... well, he still wasn't clear on exactly what he wanted. He knew what she required, however. He knew the situation would become more complicated once they became sexually intimate. Whether he wanted to admit it or not, making love with Holly would transcend the act. It would be the first step to the big *C*.

And besides sex and commitment, there was one other factor in this relationship that required some heavy-duty thought on Brooks's part. There was Zane.

Glancing in the rearview mirror again, Brooks smiled at the dark-haired boy and received the usual sunny grin in return. If ten days wasn't long enough to know whether he could make a long-term commitment to Holly, it also wasn't long enough to know if he could be a father to Zane.

But he knew how good it felt when the kid smiled at him. He knew how comfortable he had been working on Zane's homework with him these past few nights. He knew what fun they'd had last weekend playing touch football in the park and going to the movies. He knew what a charge it had given him this morning when the boy came running out of the house, calling his name, excited as all get out to see him. He was still uneasy with the idea of being anyone's hero, but he had to admit to some downright warm and fuzzy feelings when this boy looked up at him with those big, dark eyes. Just that look was enough to make a man feel pretty heroic.

Brooks wasn't blind to the potential problems with this kid. Zane was headstrong and almost too smart. As the apple of his mother's and grandmother's eyes, he had learned to twist them around to his way of thinking most of the time. If he weren't essentially good-hearted, he would be a first-class brat right now. He wasn't. Yet if something long-term did develop between Brooks and Holly, Zane might resent having the father he thought he craved.

Long-term. Father. The words buzzed in Brooks's head like a swarm of bees. Where had they come from?

One sidelong glance at Holly's profile provided the answer. This auburn-haired witch had him completely befuddled. And they hadn't even slept together. He shuddered to think what Mike would say if

Brooks told him. But the words, *extra, totally screwed,* joined the buzzing in his brain.

"Brooks," Holly said, getting his attention. "Where are we going? You've passed at least three perfectly good Christmas-tree lots."

"We're going to Elvis's."

"Graceland?"

Zane stuck his head over the seat. "They're selling trees at Elvis's house?"

Grinning, Brooks hung a right off the freeway. "Just sit tight, okay? You're going to love this place."

He sped past the white-columned mansion Elvis Presley had called home and thousands of tourists trooped through every year. A few miles down the road, in the parking lot of an empty grocery store building, he spied the sign he sought. He pointed it out to Zane, who read aloud, "No Blue Christmas, Get Your Live Trees Here."

The lot was jammed with cars. Groups of people in all sizes, shapes and colors prowled through row upon row of trees, while Elvis Presley's recording of "Blue Christmas" wafted through the clear December air.

Before they got out of the Bronco, Holly turned to Brooks with an incredulous look on her face. "A Christmas-tree lot with an Elvis theme?"

"Oh, it gets better," Brooks said, grinning. "Wait till you meet the proprietor, T. Peabody Jones."

"Who?"

"If you think the name's strange, just wait until you see him."

Holly didn't have to wait long. T. Peabody came striding out from among the trees about the time Brooks and company started into them. He wasn't someone you could miss—not with his greased, jet black pompadour wig, his bell-bottomed white jump-suit and the purple satin-lined cape draped over his shoulders.

He ripped off his sunglasses, looked at Brooks and let out a "Yee-haw!" before grabbing him up in a bear hug. And that took some doing, since T. Peabody was a foot shorter. But what he lacked in height, he made up for in girth. He twirled Brooks around with such glee that his wig shifted up to reveal his bald head.

"I de-clare," he shouted pulling the wig back in place. "Where you been, boy?"

"You know where I keep myself."

"Still walking the path of the righteous."

"Always." Brooks fixed him with his most official-looking glare. "What about you?"

Holding up beringed fingers, T. Peabody appeared insulted. He looked over each shoulder before drop-ping his booming voice to a stage whisper, "My son, how could you even ask me that? Since my last brush with the law nearly six years—"

"Four years," Brooks corrected.

"All right, all right," the man intoned with dra-matic flair. "It was four years ago. But since then, I've been a straight-arrow citizen."

"No confidence schemes? No rip-offs? No fleecing of naive widows?"

"I'm appalled, appalled that you'd mention such things." Wheeling around with a quickness surpris-ing in a man his size, he looked Holly up and down. "I'm especially upset that you would talk about my past indiscretions in the presence of such a lovely lady." T. Peabody took her hand and bowed over it with a flourish as Brooks introduced him to Holly and Zane.

Holly looked dumbfounded, but she managed a squeaky "Pleased, I'm sure."

The flamboyant man replied, "The pleasure is all mine." He cut his eyes back around to Brooks. "What's she doing with a bum like you?"

"Just lucky, I guess," Brooks quipped, then got down to business. "We're looking for a tree, of course."

T. Peabody gestured with a sweep of his cape toward the lot. "Go right ahead. They're grouped by size. Prices are marked." He leaned close to add, "For you, my friend, of course there'll be a deal."

As they struck off through the smaller trees, Holly whispered, "Where in the world did you meet this guy?"

"He was one of my first collars when I made detective, before I went into narcotics."

Zane fairly danced with excitement. "You mean he's a criminal?"

"An ex-criminal, if my sources are right. Supposedly, he hasn't run a rip-off scheme since he was brought in on the last one."

Holly stopped in the middle of a row of trees in the five-to-six-foot range. "So you brought us all the way across town to buy a Christmas tree from a con artist?"

"Ex-con artist," Brooks repeated. "And keep it down, will you? He's run a legitimate business here for the past couple of Christmases. I wouldn't want to spoil it for him."

But Holly continued to stand, shaking her head. "Oh, yeah, right. This is very legitimate, I'm sure. I bet that's why he's in that Elvis disguise."

"It's not a disguise. He always dresses that way."

"Always?" Zane asked.

"It's his trademark. That's how he ran all his scams. He got folks to believe he was Elvis." Spying a promising-looking tree, Brooks stood back to get the full impact. But when he turned to ask Holly and Zane their opinion, he found them both rooted to the same spot, openmouthed. "What is it?"

"Brooks," Zane sputtered. "That guy doesn't look much like Elvis to me."

"How would you know? Elvis died before you were born."

"But everyone knows what he looks like. He was tall—"

"And handsome," Holly added. "Even when he had gained all that weight at the end, he still had a special look about him. He was dynamic."

"But who's to say how he would look if he were alive today?"

Holly and Zane exchanged a long, considering glance. Then she said, "I doubt he would have lost twelve inches or so of height."

Brooks shrugged. "All I can say is there's a sucker born every minute, and there's at least ten suckers for every shyster like T. Peabody. Besides, his Elvis impression isn't all that bad."

To illustrate the point, a voice boomed over the loudspeaker. "For all you good folks shopping for that special tree, I'd just like to say, thank you, thank you very much."

"See," Brooks said. "Now, doesn't he sound like Elvis?"

Holly and Zane rolled with laughter. They laughed so long and so hard that they had to sit down, and it was a good ten minutes before they were worth anything as far as tree shopping. Even then, no matter what Brooks said, they each answered with a solemn, Elvis trademarked "Thank you. Thank you very much," before screaming with laughter once again. It became downright embarrassing.

After much hilarity, they finally found a tree. A nice seven-footer, exactly the height Nana Flora had ordered. They picked up a smaller one for Brooks's house and an even larger one for his parents. True to his word, T. Peabody gave Brooks all three trees for the price of one.

"I guess it pays to consort with the criminal element," Holly remarked dryly once the trees were loaded on top and in the back on the Bronco.

"You know us cops," Brooks told her. "We're on a first-name basis with all the saints and sinners."

Zane piped up with a question for Brooks while Holly fell silent. Meeting T. Peabody Jones was the first incident in days that made her really think about Brooks being a cop. They had seen each other every day, but he said little about his work. He had been paged a couple of times when they were together and had to leave in a hurry one night, but he never said why and she hadn't asked. When he came over, she watched him take off his gun and helped him stow it in the closet and away from Zane just as Papa Jake used to do. And then she forgot about it until he took it back before he left. The only strong reminder of what Brooks did had come when she checked in on Lieutenant Markowitz and his wife at the hospital. But even that had ended Wednesday, when the officer was released and sent home to recuperate.

How strange that the factor that had made her resist Brooks's appeal from the beginning didn't seem so important now. Was she deliberately ignoring a potential trouble spot, or could she be involved with this man and not have to deal with his job?

Only one thing was certain—she was already in too deep with Brooks to pull out with her heart intact. The past week and a half had been simply wonderful. Besides the time they had spent at home with Zane and Nana, there had been moments alone, special moments like last night when they'd had dinner at a romantic and expensive Italian restaurant. Then they listened to jazz in a dark, smoky club that made her feel as if they'd stepped back in time to the Roaring Twenties. Later, they had necked on her couch like two foolish teenagers. Necked and petted and almost lost control.

Sighing, remembering Brooks's hands on her body, Holly almost wished they had lost control. The cautious side of her nature knew waiting was wise. But the part of her aroused by just thinking of his touch questioned the price of wisdom.

As if he knew exactly what she was thinking, Brooks turned and gave her one of his delicious, slow grins. But his next words surprised her. "Is it okay if we take this tree to my parents?"

"Your parents?" Holly repeated, straightening in her seat like a schoolgirl caught daydreaming about her beau.

"You know, my folks. I told you I have a set."

"Well...sure, of course." Even as she agreed, Holly's mind was racing. Brooks might be acting cavalier, but she suspected this was a big deal. A man who confessed freely to running from commitment probably didn't make a habit of bringing women home to meet his parents.

And no matter how he felt, it was a very big deal to her. Looking at her worn blue jeans and pink turtleneck, she wished she was wearing something a little more flattering. She flipped down the vanity mirror on her sun shield and groaned as she saw the damage done to her hair and makeup by the brisk December wind.

"You look fine," Brooks told her.

She pulled a hairbrush and lipstick from her purse. "I'm a wreck and you know it." Out of the corner of her eye, she caught the rolling-eyed glance that passed between Brooks and her son. These two seemed to have their nonverbal communication skills down pat. It still astonished Holly how quickly their rapport had been established, and how strong it was. Yet why should that be surprising, considering it was Zane who had wanted Brooks to be part of their lives in the first place?

But did they belong together? What did Brooks really think? What would his family think of her? She was, after all, a single parent who had never married her son's father. Would they judge her harshly because of a youthful mistake? It wouldn't be the first time she had faced such censure.

Her mind was racing with questions as Brooks guided his vehicle back onto the freeway and then into a pleasant neighborhood. Only somewhat newer than the area Holly had called home most of her life, these streets were tree lined, most of the houses were well kept and the yards nicely maintained. Just as in her neighborhood, there were some signs of decay, but more signs of young families moving back in, restoring and revamping. Today's cool but beautiful weather was no doubt responsible for the people Holly saw out in their yards, decorating for Christmas or catching up on late-autumn chores.

The farther they drove, the damper Holly's palms grew. Her nerves were humming by the time Brooks turned in at a rambling brick-and-clapboard house at the end of a cul-de-sac. Cars lined the drive. Several children were chasing each other around in the yard while a tall, gray-haired man hung miniature wreaths on the charcoal-colored shutters.

"I should have known there'd be a crowd here," Brooks grumbled, half to himself. "There's not a single one of us living at home now, but this place is packed all the time."

His pained expression worried Holly. Perhaps he hadn't planned on their meeting so much of the family today. "Would you rather Zane and I wait in the car?"

Brooks laughed. "Fat chance of that." He nodded toward the house. "They'd find you."

"They" turned out to be the four women who came out on the porch and down the drive while Holly, Brooks and Zane climbed out of the Bronco. The tall woman in the center with salt-and-pepper hair was Brooks's mother, Regina. He had inherited her eyes, as well as her direct way of approaching a person. She greeted Holly and Zane as if they were old friends.

The three of his five sisters who were present were friendly, but obviously curious as they surrounded Holly. Carmen, closest in age to Brooks, was a blue-eyed blonde who worked with her father in the plumbing business. It was her three kids who were racing around the yard, and her husband, Brad, who appeared around a corner of the house just as Holly was meeting the other two sisters. Brown-eyed Peggy, a teacher, was pregnant. Mary Jane, one of the twin sisters, was tall and slim, with Brooks's coloring and the quietly elegant looks of a high-fashion model. But she was an attorney, and Holly found herself pitying the witnesses who might face her on the stand. By the time they had walked up the drive to the house, Mary Jane knew where Holly worked and lived, why she wasn't married, as well as the why and how of her meeting Brooks.

Feeling overwhelmed, Holly shot a pleading look over her shoulder toward Brooks. He and Brad were standing on either side of Zane, pity written into their expressions. Brooks made a move to rescue Holly, but his father took care of that.

"See here," he said as the group of women approached the shutter where he had wired a Christmas wreath in place. "The four of you ought to be ashamed, descending on this young woman like a school of piranha. That's probably why none of your brothers ever brings anyone to meet us."

"Dad," Carmen protested, shooting a sidelong look at Holly. "Don't be silly. Of course Brooks has brought—"

"Oh, hush," her father interrupted. "I'm sure she can tell by the way you're acting that this is a novel experience." Friendliness gleamed from his soft brown eyes as he stuck out his hand. "I'm Paul Casey. Pleased to meet you."

Smiling, Holly introduced herself and relaxed as he escorted her up on the porch and into the house. As tall as his eldest son and nearly as broad through the chest and shoulders, Paul was easy to respond to. His was the natural warmth of a born charmer.

But then, all of them were charming, she decided as the afternoon progressed. Carmen and Brad's kids took Zane in as if he were one of their own. Peggy chatted about the twins she was expecting. And even Mary Jane relaxed her cross-examination style. Regina served coffee and Christmas cookies while the men wrangled the tree from the Bronco, into a stand and into the space that had been cleared in front of the living room's corner window.

"Right where we always put it," Brooks said, accepting a mug of coffee from his mother once the tree was standing.

"It'll probably fall," Peggy predicted.

Mary Jane agreed. "Seems like it does most every year. Especially when Brooks is the one who brings it home." She cocked her head to the side as she studied the tree. "See—the trunk's crooked. It'll fall."

"Don't be such a know-it-all," Brooks retorted. "And it's not crooked."

"I am what I am," Mary Jane said. "And it is crooked."

"Is not.

"Is so."

"Stop squabbling," their mother remonstrated, as if they were still kids. She turned to Holly. "These two have been fighting for supremacy since before Mary Jane could talk."

"What about her twin?" Holly asked while the brother and sister continued their good-natured squabble.

"Moriah is as sweet as Mary Jane is spicy. They don't even look alike." Gesturing toward the kitchen, Regina added, "Come on, let me show you some pictures."

Leaving the others to see to the tree, Holly followed the older woman through the kitchen to a large family room that had obviously been added to the original house. The room jutted out into the backyard with floor-to-ceiling windows on two sides and a massive stone fireplace on the end wall. The fourth wall was covered in framed family pictures and shelves crammed with trophies, awards and various other family memorabilia.

Regina tapped a photo near the center. Standing beside a younger Mary Jane was a sandy-haired pixie, as fresh-scrubbed pretty as her twin was classically beautiful. "That's Moriah."

"She looks more like Peggy than Mary Jane."

Pointing to another brunette who favored Brooks, Regina said, "This is our other daughter, Kathleen. And these are our other boys, Mickey and Ted, named for baseball players Mantle and Williams. Paul has an obsession with the game. I had to work hard to keep him from naming one of the girls Babe Ruth Casey."

Laughing, Holly looked down at the photo of the two youngest Casey males. "They look like twins."

"But not identical. The differences are clearer in person. Eye color, hair, size."

"All these handsome children. And grandchildren, too." Holly stepped back to take in the numerous photos. "You and Brooks's father must be so proud of them."

"It's been a joy. And a struggle at times, too. I certainly didn't set out to have this many children, but they came, so we did the best we could." Regina chuckled. "People are always asking me why I didn't figure out what caused them."

"People can be rude."

"People like my own daughters."

The quiet statement made Holly look up from her study of a photo of Brooks as a boy. "No one's been rude to me."

"But they were giving you the third degree."

"If I had a brother, I'm sure I'd be concerned about who he was seeing."

"Yes, but the girls came on pretty strong. Because their father is right. Brooks hasn't brought a girlfriend home since he was in school." The blue eyes sharpened. "So I figure you're someone pretty special."

Taken aback by the straightforwardness, Holly cast about for a reply. "Mrs. Casey—"

"It's 'Regina,' dear," the older woman said, putting her hand on Holly's arm. "And I didn't mean to make you uncomfortable. Brooks's personal life is his own and none of my business, so I'm not fishing for details. But when he mentioned you to me the other night when we spoke on the phone—"

"He told you about me?"

"He told me all about you and your son."

Holly glanced down at her sneakers and decided to confront her chief worry straight away. "I guess Brooks mentioned that Zane is...well, that Zane's father and I..."

"Never married?" Regina supplied as Holly's words faded.

Lifting her chin proudly, Holly said, "Yes, that's right. I had Zane when I was nineteen, and I wasn't married."

"Well, he appears to be a terrific boy. Brooks is quite taken with him."

"I'm very proud of Zane."

Once more, Regina patted her on the arm. "As well you should be. I know how hard it is to raise children with a good man at your side. I know it takes even more strength to go it alone."

As Holly gave credit to her grandparents for their support, she found herself warming even more to this woman. Holly had half expected disapproval of the sort she had encountered in the past. She got anything but that from this delightful, open woman. In fact, Regina's next words had a distinctly encouraging sound.

"After Brooks called me the other night," she continued. "I told Paul you were important, otherwise Brooks wouldn't have said a word about you. And the fact that you're here—well, that says it all in my book."

Holly cleared her throat. She didn't want Brooks's mother to get the wrong idea. "We haven't known each other all that long. We're not...serious. I mean, Brooks isn't sure about settling down and I'm—"

The other woman waved aside her explanation. "You don't have to tell me about Brooks." She turned back to the family photos, a line appearing between her eyebrows. "Sometimes, when I think about how Paul and I raised the children, I feel that Brooks, being the oldest, got shortchanged. He and Carmen were always the ones who were asked to wait or to do without or to take care of the others. In Carmen's case, it only seemed to sharpen her need for a family of her own, she plunged right in with Brad. But for Brooks..." Sighing, she shook her head. "I've worried about his tendency to be a loner. It was always there, but it's gotten worse over the years."

"Some people are just that way. It's not necessarily a result of upbringing or family life."

"But there's so much stress in Brooks's work. At least I read that there is. He never seems to want to talk about it to any of us." Regina faced Holly again. "I hope he can talk to you."

Feeling guilty because she had, consciously or not, been avoiding talking about his work, Holly said, "He's very private."

"Do you know much about that other officer, his partner who was hurt?"

"Dan Markowitz?"

"The first I heard of it was in the paper. I recognized the officer's name, and I called Brooks. But of course, he didn't tell me anything. Then, over Thanksgiving, he was so...so morose or something..." She broke off, biting her lip. "I've been worried that something is wrong. It's just this feeling I have. But I'm probably making a mountain out of a molehill. We mothers tend to do that, don't we?"

Though Holly nodded in agreement, she was realizing Regina's maternal sixth sense was right. Brooks had opened up to Holly about the man he had killed several years ago, the problems he'd had since and his guilt over his partner's beating. But he had never pursued the subjects with her again, despite her offer to listen. And, of course, she hadn't pushed him to talk, either. On the other hand, he had already spent hours asking her about her work, how she felt about it, the frustrations and anxieties. Her selfishness shamed her.

"Holly?" Regina lightly squeezed her arm. "You look upset. I didn't mean to offend or—"

"Oh, no," Holly said, taking her hand. "I'm not upset by anything you've said. I'm just standing here thinking that I probably haven't been as sensitive to the stresses of Brooks's job as I could have been."

Regina lifted an eyebrow. "How so?"

"Just by not being ready to listen."

"Don't be too hard on yourself. Learning to talk to each other takes some time and some work. Men and women don't always speak the same language." With a wry chuckle, Regina slipped an arm around Holly's shoulders. "Lord knows, sometimes men barely speak at all."

They were laughing in agreement when Brooks appeared in the doorway. "What are you two hiding in here discussing?"

"I was looking at all these family pictures," Holly explained.

"Not the one of me lying naked on the bearskin rug." Grinning, he crossed the room to stand beside them.

His mother said, "There is no such picture of any of my children."

"Well, surely you showed her the famous Elvis moon autograph."

Before Regina could reply, there was a chorus of "Mother, where are the tree decorations?" from the living room.

The older woman sighed. "They're in the same place they've been for twenty-five years." With an apologetic smile, she excused herself, leaving Brooks and Holly alone.

He pointed to a frame halfway down the wall. Sure enough, "With all my best, Elvis Presley" was scrawled on a scrap of paper that had been mounted on a drawing of a full, yellow moon.

"I know it says Elvis," Holly told Brooks with a mischievous smile. "But don't you think this could really be T. Peabody Jones?"

Laughing, he said he didn't think T. Peabody had been operating his scams back then. "Besides, that would spoil the story, don't you think? Especially since Dad likes to say that was the night I was conceived, right under that moon after Elvis went on his way."

"And what does your mother say?"

"I don't think any of us have ever had the nerve to ask her."

Laughing again, Holly slipped her arm through Brooks's. "You were right, you know. You've got an absolutely terrific family."

"They're nosy and make no apologies for it." He put both arms around her, bringing her close as he kissed her nose. "I hope they haven't scared you off."

"Are you kidding? I'm fascinated by all the personalities."

"They're pretty fascinated by you."

"You don't sound pleased."

"Well, it means a lot of activity in the coming weeks. They'll all be calling me, and then you and I will be asked over for dinner at all the houses here in Memphis, where we'll undergo even closer inspection. And when Kathleen and Moriah and the boys show up for Christmas, you'll get the third degree again. And so will I."

"I'm sorry."

Brooks smiled down at her. "It's okay. I think you're worth it." He lifted his hand and ran a fingertip over her lips. "If you want to know the truth, I think you're downright fascinating myself."

"Is that so?"

His voice grew husky as his head dipped nearer. "Mysteries have always intrigued me."

"I feel like I'm pretty much an open book."

"But there are chapters we've yet to explore," he whispered just before kissing her.

Holly wondered if she could ever tire of the headiness of his kisses, and she had real questions about how much longer either of them were going to be able to hold out without making love. "This waiting game," she murmured against his lips. "I think I'm getting tired of it."

He nibbled on her ear. "Me, too."

"So let's take Zane home."

"And go to my place."

"Sounds good."

Taking a step back, Brooks said, "Are you sure?"

Try as she might, her voice wouldn't remain level as she replied, "Positively sure."

He gripped her hands and brought them up to his lips. "I want it to be right, Holly."

"Then it will be."

Her serenity was what struck Brooks the most. She looked like an angel, standing there with her face so composed, her eyes brimming with a mixture of eagerness and trust. He supposed his sudden, impatient urge to get an angel naked would qualify as blasphemy in his mother's house, but he didn't care. All he wanted was to be alone with Holly as soon as possible, to explore every curve of her body, to bury himself deep in her sweet, welcoming female form.

"Let's go get that boy of yours," he said, pulling her toward the living room.

Everything took so much time. Saying goodbye to his family. Driving to Holly's. Unloading the tree. Finding an explanation for Nana Flora as to why they didn't want to do the decorations tonight. Convincing Zane that he didn't want to come with them. Then they had to drive to Brooks's house, halfway across town.

It was dusk before they pulled up outside the renovated bungalow near Memphis University. His unmarked police sedan was parked in his drive, so he pulled in behind it. The street was quiet, with no traffic. Christmas lights bloomed in most of the windows.

Holly studied his white, green-shuttered house with approval. "I like it."

"Even though I've been living here five years, it still needs work. I never seem to have the time. And it's a mess inside. I wasn't exactly expecting company."

She turned to smile at him. "I'm not really interested in your housekeeping."

He resisted the urge to whistle as he climbed out of his vehicle. He had almost forgotten his Christmas tree was sticking out the back, and he would have preferred not to fool with it now. But he was reluctant to leave the Bronco open that way. Holly helped him pull the tree out. He carried it to the porch and stood it against the wall before he unlocked the front door.

"Let me just disarm the alarm system," he said, pushing the door open.

"I guess I could expect a cop to have an alarm."

"Nothing can keep out someone who wants in bad enough, but this is a start." Brooks quickly punched in the alarm code on the control pad near the door, then turned to usher Holly inside.

But before he could, his Bronco exploded in a ball of fire.

Chapter Seven

Holly was freezing. Temperatures had plunged as the December night had fallen, and she had been huddled on the front steps of Brooks's neighbor's house for at least an hour and a half. The kindly older couple, who were no doubt as frightened as she was, had asked her to come inside. But she preferred to stay here, where Brooks had brought her.

After the Bronco her son had been in all day blew up.

Shivering, she crossed her arms over her chest and tried not to think about what *could* have happened. The reality was bad enough. For perhaps the twentieth time since the car went up in flames, she ran through the events in her head. She had just stepped into Brooks's house when the boom of the explosion hit. Brooks had thrown her to the floor, covering her body with his before she knew what happened. In the distance, she heard a car speed away, and then Brooks was dragging her up with him and into the house, where he called the police.

And now the street, so quiet when she and Brooks had arrived for their romantic evening, was now bedlam. In the surrealistic glow of blue lights, high-beamed flashlights and street lamps, fire trucks and police cars blocked all traffic. Neighbors who weren't in their homes or being interviewed by policemen were gathered in groups on the sidewalks or in their yards. In Brooks's driveway, the fire around the Bronco was out, and technicians were already prowling through the burned-out shells of the Bronco and his departmental vehicle, which had been parked in front of it. The siding on the front and left of his house was scorched, and it was probably a minor miracle that the house hadn't caught fire. A team of men and women had been inside Brooks's house for a while now.

Probably making sure there weren't any more bombs.

Holly inhaled sharply, trying to control the trembling that seized her. She was concentrating so hard that she jumped when she felt a touch on her shoulder. Looking up, she found Brooks's friend, Detective Donna Fortnoy, whom Holly had met just a little earlier with her partner, Mike DeWitt.

"You look like you could use this," the petite brunette said, holding out a blanket.

Mumbling her gratitude, Holly stood, took the blanket and wrapped it around herself. Then she sat down on the steps again.

Donna joined her. "I could take you home if you want."

"I want to see Brooks."

"He may be busy for a while."

After studying the other woman's noncommittal expression for a moment, Holly said, "Can you tell me anything about what's going on?"

"Sure." The detective pointed to the squad around the cars. "They're trying to determine what kind of bomb it was." She nodded toward the house. "Everyone in there is—"

"I know why they're in there," Holly cut in. "I know all that. What I want to know is why this happened."

Donna cleared her throat. "We're not sure. Brooks will be able to tell you more later."

"But someone's after him. This wasn't random, was it?"

"I don't know—"

"Don't treat me like the dumb girlfriend." Holly was alarmed at how her voice rose, at its hysterical edge. "I think I have a right to know. If that bomb had gone off just a minute earlier, just a half a minute, I would... and Brooks would..."

"Hey, hey," Donna said, reaching out to grip her arm. "I'm not patronizing you. I just can't tell you why. We're not sure why."

Holly drew the blanket tighter around her shoulders and shrank back against the step, trying to regain her equilibrium. "I'm sorry, Donna. I didn't mean to snap at you. I'm just so worried. My son was in that car today." She sucked in her breath again as a new thought hit her. "I need to call my son, let him and my grandmother know that we're okay. If this gets on any newscast before I call—''

''They've already been told something of what happened and that you're okay,'' Donna assured her. ''A couple of units were dispatched to your house right away.''

Alarmed rather than comforted, Holly demanded, ''Why to my house?''

Donna looked as though she regretted speaking. ''It was a precaution Brooks wanted. Other units went to his parents' home, as well. He was afraid he'd been followed all day today.''

The scene in front of Holly started to whirl and darken, and quickly, she ducked her head down toward her knees as she gulped in air. She had never fainted in her life, not even when she first faced the blood and gore of a busy E.R. But she had never faced anything quite like this. That was work. This was her life.

''Are you okay?'' Donna asked.

Holly didn't answer. Glancing up, she saw Brooks walk down his drive and speak to one of the technicians working on the Bronco. What he heard must have distressed him, because he stepped back and stalked off, head bowed, rubbing a hand over his face. He was joined by Donna's partner, Mike, as well as a tall black man who had introduced himself to Holly as Captain Dixon. The three men engaged in an animated discussion. At least Brooks was animated. Mike just stood to the side with his arms crossed, and Dixon merely shook his head.

Tired of watching, wondering and worrying, Holly threw off the blanket and stood, ignoring Donna's warning as she ran across the yard. Two other officers made a grab for her, but she dodged them, as well. Their shouts brought Brooks wheeling around, and Holly ran right into his arms, just as someone, Donna probably, yelled, "Hold your fire!"

"My God," Brooks muttered. His heart was racing beneath her cheek as she grabbed hold of him. He pulled her away, gripping her shoulders as he stared down at her with eyes that looked enormous in his white, tense face. "What are you trying to do, Holly, get yourself killed?"

"You tell me. Isn't that what almost happened with the car? Couldn't we have been killed then?"

"But we weren't. We're okay. And I'll explain everything later."

"I want to know now," she said. "I was in that car, Brooks. Me and Zane were in that car."

With a strangled oath, Brooks pulled her tight against his chest again. She was right, of course. She and Zane could have been killed. For that, she deserved an answer. And he would give it to her. "I promise I'll explain it all soon. I want you to go home, and as soon as I can, I'll call—"

"Call?" she repeated, pushing him away. "You'll call *soon?* Am I supposed to accept that after what's happened here tonight?"

"Casey." Captain Dixon's voice made Brooks turn. "I think you need to attend to your personal business and leave everything else to us tonight."

"But how can I do that?" Brooks retorted, pivoting back to him. "This is Dante, and he's after me. So I say I put myself out there for him to find. We make a meeting with him, serve me up and you bust him."

Holly gasped, but Brooks determinedly ignored her.

Dixon just shook his head. "How could you be any more 'out there' than you've been? It's just like we discussed before, if he wanted you dead, you'd be dead."

"Well, this was awful damn close. To me and to..." Brooks swallowed, again looking at Holly. "To me and too many innocent bystanders." He made a sweeping gesture with his hands. "A street full of innocent people."

"The experts say they already know it was a remote-controlled bomb," Dixon continued, as if Brooks hadn't even spoken. "Someone in the car you heard speed away probably set it off when they saw you and Miss MacPherson go in the house. The charge was just big enough to make a lot of bang and some fire. Any more serious damage would have probably been an accident."

"I didn't see a car," Brooks muttered. He hadn't seen it because all his attention had been focused on Holly. He hadn't even noticed if they'd been followed today. And not paying attention to what was going on around him could be a cop's final, fatal error.

Mike spoke up, "No one else saw a car, either, Brooks. We've canvased the whole street now."

Donna, who had joined the group, added, "Everyone heard the explosion. A few people heard the car drive away. But no one got a look at it."

"So we've got nothing again," Dixon said, matter-of-factly closing the small notebook he carried. "That seems to be Dante's stock-in-trade, doesn't it?"

"But this was him," Brooks growled. "He wants me because I killed his son."

Dixon's only reply was a grunt. "I've got some other theories, Casey, but I'm not too crazy about discussing them while all this commotion is going on."

"Then let's get back to the precinct."

"I think you ought to get Miss MacPherson home."

"But I shouldn't be near her." Beside Brooks, Holly made a low sound of protest. He knew when she had time to think about this she would agree he needed to stay as far from her and Zane as he could. But right now, she just looked hurt.

Dixon glanced at her, then swung his gaze back to Brooks and glared. Walking away, he gestured for Brooks to follow him. "Listen," he said, once they were some distance from the others. "Does this woman mean anything to you, Casey?"

Brooks was startled. He and his captain rarely discussed anything personal. "Sir, I don't see where that has any bearing—"

"Just answer the question."

Jaw squaring, Brooks said, "I think she does, sir."

"You *think?*" Dixon echoed, snorting in disgust.

Brooks resisted the urge to tell his boss what he could do with his meddling. But all he said was, "I want her protected. To do that, I've got to stay away from her."

"Then we'll keep you away. We'll keep you as far away as possible. But first, I'm sending her home in a car, and you're going with her. After what she's been through tonight, she's owed some explanations, and some of your time and consideration."

"But, sir—"

Dixon held up a hand to stop the protest. "Dante isn't going to come after you again tonight, Casey. He may be an arrogant cuss, but he's not stupid. He's not about to ambush the fleet of patrol cars I'm going to send with you and Miss MacPherson. And from some pieces of information I received just before your little explosion here, he's got bigger business than you coming up in the near future. Playing with you is just a sideline.''

''Why? What have you heard?''

''Take your lady home first,'' Dixon said with the sort of finality Brooks knew from experience he couldn't combat. ''When you know she and her family and your family are okay, Mike'll bring you in. We're going to put you somewhere that Dante won't look.''

''But I want him to look for me. That's how we'll find him.''

Ignoring Brooks, Dixon just strode away, snapping out orders to a patrolman standing nearby and pausing for a few moments to say something to Holly that Brooks couldn't hear.

Half an hour later, after a silent, tension-filled ride, Brooks and Holly were in front of her house. Brooks made sure there were two patrolmen waiting to escort them before he allowed Holly to climb out of the back seat after him. When she did, Zane burst through the front door, calling her name. Seeing the boy running across the yard, right out in the open where any lunatic could take a shot at him, Brooks's heart froze. But, thank God, his reflexes didn't.

With two giant-size steps, he met Zane, then swept him up, shielding the sturdy young body with his own as he made for the porch. Holly called his name, but Brooks knew she was fine with the two officers on either side of her and Mike's car pulling up at the curb. The most important thing, the only thing he could think about, was getting her son in the house and out of any possible harm's way.

An overreaction? Maybe. But for Brooks, it was pure instinct. When he reached the front foyer where Nana Flora was waiting, he couldn't stop hugging Zane. He told himself he would have reacted the same way with any kid in the same situation. But with another kid, would fear be squeezing his gut as it was now? Would tears, actual, for-real tears, be pricking the back of his eyes?

The older woman standing near the stairway with her hands clasped was looking at him intently, as if she could see straight into the secrets of his heart. But he didn't want those secrets revealed, not even to himself. He simply couldn't open that door right now. All that mattered was that Zane, *his little man,* Holly's boy, was safe and sound.

"You're choking me," the boy said, squirming in his grip.

Brooks had to let him go. "I'm sorry." His legs felt kind of weak, so he slid to his knees in front of Zane. "I'm really sorry."

Steps pounding across the front porch made him turn. Holly raced inside, breathing hard, as Zane ran into her arms. "Do you want to tell me what that was all about?" she demanded of Brooks.

Bowing his head, Brooks took a couple of deep breaths and tried to clear his head. Holly and Zane were silhouetted in the lights from outside. They stood together, but cops crowded the doorway behind them, and the sight of those uniforms filled Brooks with an overpowering sense of frustration and guilt. He had done this, placed them in possible jeopardy, and now he had to set it right. After that, then maybe...just maybe...

He closed his mind to any possibilities. He had no time to sort through the complexities of his feelings for this woman and boy. That was the problem with these sorts of emotions. They took too much time, too much thought. And right now, he needed all his brainpower for his job.

But Holly wasn't letting him go to that job so easily. She closed the door on the policemen on the porch, then faced Brooks with a determined expression. "It's time to talk."

After Zane and Nana Flora were reassured and sent upstairs, Holly made Brooks sit down. He didn't want to. He wanted to rush through an explanation and get back to his precinct office. Mike had left, but he was awaiting Brooks's call to take him to the precinct office. But Holly wasn't letting Brooks hurry. Dixon had told her to make Brooks explain what was going on and to try to calm him down.

Holly had no idea why the big, imposing captain thought she would have any impact on the impatient, angry man who had grabbed Zane and raced into the house like a soldier fleeing a missile hit. She also had no clue why she had believed Dixon when he had told her, "It will be okay. If Brooks will just keep his cool, this will be fine."

Yet she did believe him, and she was going to try to do as he had asked in regard to Brooks.

So first she made Brooks sit down and call his parents to see that they were okay and to reassure them about his own safety. Then she insisted Brooks re-hash what he had already told her about the death of Dante Wilson's son. She learned of Dante's supposed return to Memphis, about how his initials had been on a note addressed to Brooks and left with Markowitz's beaten body. Added to that was tonight's explosion. To Brooks, all this meant Dante was out for blood. His blood.

Holly wasn't so sure.

"You're not?" Brooks said, sitting up in his seat in amazement. "How can you disagree?"

"Because Dixon's right when he says you should already be dead if that were this Dante's intent." *At least, she hoped, she prayed, he was right.*

Brooks pushed impatiently away from the table. "Dixon doesn't know this guy the way I do."

"So you really know Dante? Know how he thinks?"

"I've chased him ever since I got into narcotics."

"Then hasn't Dixon been chasing him, as well?"

Brooks swept that question aside with an impatient gesture as he stood. "Dixon's also got some other theory about what's going on." He glanced at his watch. "Since I've told you everything I know, I need to get out of here and go hear about that theory."

She needed to stall him. "First you should eat something." Her voice sounded calmer than she felt.

"I'm not hungry."

He couldn't leave. She couldn't let him leave. "It's nearly ten o'clock, and you haven't eaten since we had an early lunch here today."

"I'll grab something out of a machine down at the precinct."

She pointed to the chair. "Sit down. You're not leaving here without some decent food in you."

Hands on hips, powerful legs planted wide apart, Brooks studied her in silence.

"Stop trying to intimidate me with that hard-nosed cop look."

"Holly—"

"Sit down, Brooks," she said, a slight tremble in her voice. *What if he was right and Dixon was wrong? What if no one could protect him from Dante?* Those thoughts put force back into her command that he sit immediately.

He gave her a long look before he complied.

With a growing sense of desperation, she went to the refrigerator, got out sandwich makings and spread them on the table. Brooks was quiet as she took plates and silverware from the cabinets. Her hands shook so that the cups rattled in their saucers, but she managed to pour the coffee Nana Flora had prepared and get it to the table. Picking up a knife, she began to slice a tomato for the sandwich.

"You have to eat," she kept fussing to Brooks over and over as she cut into the tomato. "You just have to have some . . . thing." To her dismay, her voice broke in the middle of the word.

"Holly, don't," Brooks implored. "Just sit down, please. Let's talk."

Yes, they could talk. About his job. About the things she had avoided talking about before now.

"Let's talk before I have to go."

No. The word was a silent scream in her head. And suddenly it didn't matter that she had believed what Dixon told her about things being fine. She couldn't trust that. *And Brooks couldn't go. Not unless she had a guarantee he would come back. God, when had her feelings for him become this strong?*

"Holly, stop it."

Though she tried to protest, the knife slipped from her fingers and clattered to the floor.

Like lightning, Brooks was up and around the table, pulling her into his arms. "Don't. Please, please, don't cry."

She fought those tears harder than anything she had ever fought in her life. She fought and she won, because she didn't want to cry in front of him. She didn't want him to know she was scared out of her mind. Her hands curled into fists as she clenched at his soft denim shirt. She took a deep breath. He smelled like smoke and Christmas-tree sap. And he felt so solid, like a rock planted in the ground. Surely no one could hurt him.

"Don't worry," he whispered against her ear. "Promise me you won't worry."

"I can't do that."

He combed a hand through her hair, murmuring her name. "I wanted tonight to be so different, Holly, so special. I'm sorry."

"When this is over..."

Stepping away, he said, "We'll talk, when this is over."

"I'll hold you to that." She slipped her arms around him again.

"But I have to go now."

She stepped aside while he grasped the phone and punched in a number. When he hung up, there was an immediate ring back, and he asked Mike to come get him.

Holly shut her eyes momentarily, her throat constricting again before she followed Brooks out into the foyer.

"Please be careful," he told her. "They'll keep up the patrols here at your house."

"Where are you going to be?"

He laughed dryly. "Dixon says I'm going to disappear for a while, so that's probably how it will go. But don't be concerned. Call Donna, Mike or Dixon if you get frightened or anything unusual happens. And tell Zane to be extracareful at school, particularly if somebody he doesn't know approaches him."

"I know how to stay away from strangers."

Turning around, Holly saw that her son had edged down the stairs. He stood on the first landing, his brow furrowed. "What's going on, Brooks?"

Holly watched Brooks swallow hard, but he summoned a grin for Zane. "I'm going to be tied up for the next few days," he told the boy.

"Because your car burned?" That was all they had really told him—that the Bronco had caught fire.

"Sort of. It's pretty complicated."

But as he came the rest of the way downstairs, Zane still looked confused. "Why do Mom and I have to be careful?"

Brooks shot Holly a helpless look. Placing a hand on her son's shoulder, she decided to give him at least part of the truth. "Someone who has a grudge against

Brooks may be trying to hurt him. He's worried, so he wants us to be extracareful, too."

"Can't you just arrest this guy?" Zane asked Brooks.

"It's not that easy. I wish—" The doorbell chimed before Brooks could continue.

Holly opened the door for Mike. After nodding to her and meeting Zane, he said to Brooks, "You ready to go?"

"I think so." Sighing in frustration, Brooks hunkered down in front of Zane. "Just be careful, okay? Look out for your mom and Nana Flora. If anything happens, you can always get help." He glanced up at Mike. "Since I may not be around, you can always call Lieutenant Mike here."

"Absolutely," Mike said, with a friendly smile for the boy. "Any friend of Brooks is a friend of mine."

Zane nodded, then stuck out his hand to Brooks.

Mustering a slight laugh, Brooks shook the youngster's hand, then ruffled his hair and finally, hugged him hard. Only then did he glance at Holly again.

"Take care," she said as brightly as she could.

"I will." Standing, he took her hand and brushed a kiss across her cheek, a most unsatisfactory kiss.

"I'll see you soon?" She hadn't intended that to come out as a question, maybe because she knew instinctively that Brooks wouldn't answer her. And he didn't. With a last goodbye, he walked out the door.

Wide-eyed, Mike watched him go, then caught Holly's gaze, looking uncannily like a very surprised bassett hound. "Don't worry," he offered rather ineptly.

She just nodded, and then he left, too.

Zane came to stand beside her. "This is bad, isn't it, Mom?"

The last thing she wanted was to frighten her son. So Holly got a grip on herself. She was forgetting what Captain Dixon had told her. She had to hold on to that. "No, it's not bad. Brooks just has to take care of some stuff. He won't get to help us decorate the tree like he planned."

From the staircase behind them, Nana Flora asked, "So he's gone?" Her normally cheery expression was grave.

"I'm sorry," Holly said. "I should have called you down so you could say goodbye."

"It's okay. I'll see him soon, won't I?"

Though she nodded, Holly felt her cheerful mask beginning to slip.

Gaze sharpening, Nana came all the way down into the foyer. "I know there's been a problem, Holly, a serious problem, but you haven't—"

Holly cut her off with a sweep of her hand. "I'll explain it to you tomorrow, Nana. Tonight—" she swallowed "—tonight, I just want to go to bed."

"But, Holly," Nana protested. "There are still police cars outside."

"They'll be there a little while. It's just a precaution."

"But why?"

"Nana, please," Holly snapped, her patience at an end. "Just don't worry. Brooks said not to worry. So let's all just go to bed." Dropping a kiss on Zane's cheek, Holly sped upstairs. She couldn't stand it another minute, couldn't stand not to show how very worried she was. She was so worried and so angry, too. Angry for letting herself care for this man, for placing her heart on the line.

In Mike's car, Brooks stared silently out at the familiar Memphis cityscape. The lights of downtown brightened the dark sky. He wished something could lighten the darkness inside of him. He had hated that last little scene with Holly. He hated feeling guilty because she was scared. Lord in heaven, how had he gotten into this?

"So tell me about Holly," Mike said, breaking into Brooks's thoughts.

"Nothing to tell."

His friend laughed, and Brooks glared at his profile. "What did that mean?"

"Just that you're swimming in a river in Egypt, Brooks, my man. De-nial." Chuckling again, Mike shook his head.

"And you need some new material," Brooks grumbled, sliding down in his seat with his arms crossed.

Mike fell silent for a moment, and when he spoke again, there was nothing teasing about his tone. "It's not necessarily a bad thing, you know."

"What?"

"Being with someone."

"Yeah, right."

"You might actually find out you need someone."

This time, Brooks's only reply was a grunt.

"It looks to me like Holly and her kid kind of need you."

"I didn't ask for your advice," Brooks snapped.

"But I think you need it."

"And you're such an expert on relationships? Since when?"

That shut Mike up, but it didn't make Brooks feel any better, and judging by way the car picked up speed, he had really upset Mike. "I'm sorry," Brooks offered after the silence between them had stretched for too long. "I didn't mean to say that about you and relationships. I know you and Patty have been having some rough times."

"Yeah, we have," Mike muttered. "And maybe because of that, because we've actually started talking about some things, maybe I've learned something that could help you."

"Like what?"

"Like sometimes the thing you've thought was true turns out to be a lie."

"What does that mean?"

"Just think about yourself, Brooks. As long as I've known you, you've avoided getting really involved with anyone."

"Yeah, and I was smart," Brooks said, thinking again of the way he had left Holly and Zane, the way they had looked at him.

"But now you're involved with this woman."

A denial sprang to Brooks's lips, but he didn't say it. Why should he? This man knew him far too well to believe it.

"You're involved with her and her son," Mike continued. "And for the last week or so, you've seemed pretty happy about it."

"How do you know? I don't remember telling you much about them."

Mike gave a short laugh. "After all these years, don't you think Donna and I know you well enough to see when you're happy? Hell, you stopped biting people's heads off. You acted like there was actually a life besides the work."

"Well, that was a mistake," Brooks retorted. "I haven't been paying attention. And now look what happened."

"Jeez, Brooks. That would have happened anyway. Are you trying to say that before you got yourself tangled up with this lady, you regularly checked under your car for bombs?"

"No, but—"

"But nothing." Swinging the car onto the street in front of the precinct, Mike made a sound of disgust. "All I'm trying to tell you is that you shouldn't blow Holly off."

Brooks was startled. "Why do you think I was going to do that?"

"Weren't you?"

He didn't answer.

"That's what I thought," Mike said. "As soon as all this mess with Dante gets cleared up, you're planning to back off from Holly. That's a mistake."

"And why are you so all-fired interested in my personal life?" Brooks was beginning to get hot. Though they were friends, Mike had never talked to him this way before.

"I just don't want to see a friend mess up a good thing."

"You don't even know Holly," Brooks snapped. "You don't know if she's good for me or not."

Mike pulled the car to a stop under a streetlight in the parking lot beside the precinct building. Brooks could see his grin. "Oh, I got a gut feeling about her."

"Your gut may be full of beans."

"My instincts are pretty damn good, thank you very much. So you ought to be listening."

Brooks exhaled in frustration. "Let's just get inside, okay?"

"Wait a minute," Mike said before Brooks could reach for the door handle. He looked dead serious. "A couple of weeks back, you said something to me. You asked me if I could live without Patty as opposed to this job."

Brooks remembered that night, just after he and Holly had coffee and he kissed her for the first time. Mike had come into the office, upset over the state of his marriage.

"Well," Mike continued, "you really made me think, Brooks. Bottom line is I can't live without her."

"But can she live with this job?"

"You mean, is she making me choose?"

"Yeah."

"She doesn't work that way."

"So what are you going to do?"

"Be a little more flexible, a little more open with her." He grimaced. "God, can you believe it's me saying that?"

"I'm glad you two are working it out," Brooks said. "But what's this got to do with me and Holly?"

"Just that you have to ask yourself the same question you put to me. Can you live without her?"

The words ripped through Brooks like a bullet. He actually flinched. And he couldn't confront them. "God, Mike, don't be asking me that. Holly and I, we're not . . . not to that point, you know. We haven't even . . ." He swallowed. "I haven't even slept with her."

Mike's eyes narrowed. Then he smiled. A big, goofy smile. "Is that so?"

"Yeah, it is," Brooks replied, challenging him to say anything derogatory.

"If that's the case, this is even more serious than I thought."

Swearing, Brooks jerked open the door and stepped out, forgetting he might be a hit man's target, forgetting everything but how aggravated his friend's smug look made him.

Mike caught up to him as they swung into the precinct doors. "I wasn't criticizing," he said, following Brooks to the stairway.

"I don't give a damn what you think."

"I didn't sleep with Patty till we got married."

That admission made Brooks falter a moment on the steps. Then he surged ahead, pausing only at the door to the second floor. He turned to face Mike. "Do me a favor, will you?"

"Anything."

"Dixon's going to put me away somewhere for a while."

"Probably for the best."

"But while I'm gone…" Brooks stopped to clear his throat, letting his gaze skitter away from his friend's. "While I'm gone, check on Holly and Zane. Just drop in, see how they are."

There was a world of understanding in the other man's puppy-dog eyes. He stuck out his hand and grasped Brooks's. "You bet, buddy."

The assurance eased something in Brooks's chest. But he didn't stop to analyze the feeling before he took a deep breath and went through the doors to face his captain.

Chapter Eight

Something was wrong with Brooks.

Zane knew it, though everyone was saying it wasn't so. His mom kept telling him everything was fine. Nana Flora denied there was a problem and told him to go play whenever he asked. But Zane could feel the trouble in the air, the same way he could walk into class at school and tell when almost everyone had messed up on a test. Adults always had a strange look about them when something was wrong. Even when they smiled, they couldn't hide it.

And his mom wasn't even bothering to smile.

Saturday night, she went to bed and left all kinds of food out in the kitchen to spoil. Sunday, she helped him and Nana Flora decorate the Christmas tree, but she didn't put Christmas music on or sing or dance around with tinsel as she usually did. And when

Wondercat tried to climb the tree, as he did every year, she didn't even yell. Monday, she came home from work and went right to bed. Tuesday, at dinner she didn't ask him about his Knights' class, something she always did. But worst of all, on Wednesday she didn't go to work.

For as long as Zane could remember, his mom had told him her work was so important and there were so many people counting on her that the only time she could stay home was when there was an emergency, like the time he and Nana had both caught the flu. So the sight of her sitting in the kitchen in her robe Wednesday morning was a real surprise. She was usually on her way out by the time he got dressed. Zane heard her tell Nana that she had called Mrs. Coulter last night and asked for a few days off, "To clear my head."

What was wrong with her head?

The only thing Zane could see wrong was that Brooks wasn't here. But he'd said he'd see them soon, hadn't he? Zane couldn't remember exactly. The only thing clear to him about Saturday night was the way Brooks grabbed him up and ran him into the house, and the way he'd hugged him. Real tight. Exactly the way his mom or grandmother hugged when he had spent the night with a friend, or done something good in school. Brooks's hug had made Zane feel especially good. He knew his quest was almost over. Brooks and his mom were always kissing and laughing together. Because of that, Marcus and his other buddies who had moms *and* dads said Zane could probably count on Brooks being his dad real soon.

*But maybe there was something Zane didn't know.
Like maybe Brooks was gone, the same way his Papa
Jake was gone. Forever.*

That thought hit Zane just as he laid his books on
the desk in his room Wednesday afternoon. A knot
hard as a rock filled his belly at the thought of Brooks
being gone for good. Shrugging out of his jacket, he
threw it on the floor and raced downstairs, calling for
his mom.

"I'm in here," she said from the living room.

Zane found her sitting beside the Christmas tree,
wrapping packages. That looked so normal, *she*
looked so normal, that he drew up short.

"What's wrong?" she asked.

"Nothing."

"You sure?"

He tucked his hands in his pockets and tried to look
as if he didn't care. "I was just wondering if you had
talked to Brooks."

Zane was instantly sorry he asked, because his
mom's face twisted in a funny way before she shook
her head. "But he'll call soon, I'm sure," she said.

"Where is he?"

"He told you, Zane. He's working."

Watching her cut a length of wrapping paper, Zane
had another thought. "You like Brooks, don't you,
Mom?"

"Very much."

"I mean, you didn't kiss him and stuff, just because I liked him, did you?"

She put down the paper. "Of course not."

"So you didn't send him away?"

She gave him a long, long look. "Where did you get an idea like that?"

"I was just thinking about him not being here."

"He'll be back."

Swallowing past a sudden king-size lump in his throat, Zane asked, "Are you sure?"

His mother made one of those I'm-smiling-so-you-won't-know-something's-wrong smiles. "I'm positive. You stop worrying about Brooks. Christmas is in a week and half. Shouldn't you be thinking about that?"

Zane didn't answer. *Who could think about a bunch of dumb old presents when everything felt so wrong around here?*

Nana Flora came into the living room with some spools of ribbon. "Zane, you need to feed Wondercat. And there's some fresh cookies cooling out in the kitchen."

"I'm not hungry," he mumbled.

Holly reached out for him. "Are you getting sick?"

"He does look a little peaked," Nana added.

Zane backed away from them. "Can't a guy just not be hungry?"

His mom gave him another of those long looks of hers. "It's not like you to turn down cookies."

"Well, I don't want any," he retorted as hatefully as he could.

Nana Flora clucked. "Don't talk so mean to your mother."

Immediately contrite, Zane mumbled, "I'm sorry." Then he sprinted out of the living room, not even caring that his mom and grandmother continued talking about him being sick. He wasn't sick. He was just sick and tired of being lied to. If Brooks was really okay, then why didn't he call?

Instead of heading for the kitchen, Zane went to the front door and eased it open quietly, hoping his mom wouldn't hear. Ever since Saturday, when Brooks left and those police cars started parking out on the street, she'd been funny about him playing in the front yard, and she'd made him promise he wouldn't even go over to his friends' houses without asking. But no one said a word today as Zane eased outside.

Waving to the officers in the police car, Zane sat down on the steps, where the afternoon sun made it especially warm. He hoped it would get cold before Christmas, that they'd have snow. But that had never happened before, and it probably wouldn't this time. He figured it was going to be a crummy Christmas, anyway.

A familiar car pulled into the drive. Big and tan and ugly, Zane recognized it easily. "Brooks!" he shouted, getting up and racing down the front walk.

But it wasn't Brooks at all. It was that friend of his, Lieutenant Mike, who had stopped by every night since Brooks had left.

"You're in Brooks's car," Zane said, sliding to a halt in front of Mike.

"All our cars look just alike, son."

Zane gritted his teeth, trying hard not to show how disappointed he was. But he figured Lieutenant Mike knew, 'cause he looked at him kind of hard, and he put his hand on Zane's shoulder. But Brooks had said Zane should trust Mike, so maybe Mike would be straight with him.

"Brooks is not coming back, is he?"

"Who said that?" Mike demanded.

"Nobody. I just know."

"Well, I don't know it."

"Have you seen him?"

"Yeah."

"He's okay?"

"He misses you and your mom."

Zane felt the pain inside him thaw a little. "Are you sure?"

"I wouldn't lie to you."

"Then why doesn't he come see us?"

Mike's fingers lightly squeezed Zane's shoulder. His gaze was serious as he said, "Didn't Brooks explain some of that to you?" He nodded toward the nearby police car.

"Somebody might want to hurt him."

"And if it happened here, somebody else could get hurt. Somebody like you or your grandmother or your mother."

"But my mom…" Biting his lower lip, Zane glanced back toward the house. "My mom's not doing too good."

Mike nodded. "I know."

"Couldn't she go see Brooks?"

"I don't think—"

"But you said he missed her."

"Yes, but—"

"She wouldn't have to stay long. And Brooks would take care of her. I know he would."

Settling back against the car with his arms crossed, Mike let out a long breath.

Zane, who knew all about negotiations from long practice with his mom and grandmother, was sure he had scored some points. He moved in for the kill, using his best pleading face and voice as he looked up. "Please, Lieutenant Mike. I know you can do something, can't you?"

Mike made no promises. In fact, he made no reply before walking Zane up the front steps and into the house. Yet for some reason, Zane got the distinct impression that Mike was giving his request some thought. Some serious thought.

So maybe Zane's Daddy Quest wasn't stalled, after all.

The Mississippi River glowed red in the rays of the late-afternoon sun. It was a beautiful sight, particularly from the vantage point of the luxury high rise where Brooks was staying. He was in the million-dollar penthouse of a billion-dollar building hovering over the river and the tourist and business developments that crowded the banks. Brooks had to admit this was the last place anyone would think to look for an underpaid police detective.

Dixon had made the arrangements. It seemed he was tight with someone in this building's management company. This apartment, owned by a corporation, was occupied just a month out of the year and never unexpectedly. Only a special key gained anyone admittance to the top floors, and this particular floor, the top, was accessed only from separate stairs and an elevator from the floor below. Anyone getting past the security in the entrance foyer and up here would have performed a miracle. So Brooks was safe.

Safe and sound and going out of his mind.

To his way of thinking Dixon was taking some big precautions over someone whose life he didn't believe was in jeopardy. Dixon's theory was that Dante wasn't out to kill Brooks at all. Recent undercover information had revealed a rival crime family was gearing up for a major war with Dante's operation. Some minor-league dealers had finally talked. Dante had put the squeeze on them—join his team or get out of town. Dante was indeed talking big about bringing Brooks down, but Dixon believed that was all smoke, a diversion to impress his underlings and throw the police off the scent of what he was really up to, which was a takeover of all the narcotics traffic in the city. For when he made that move, the body count could be high and innocent people could be caught in the transfer of power.

"But I won't be in on it," Brooks muttered, pacing away from the panoramic view from the penthouse windows. No doubt, if a drug war broke out, Brooks would be up here, surrounded by silk and leather, marble and mahogany.

The doorbell chimed, as esthetically pleasing as the rest of the decor. But Brooks grasped his gun before moving silently across the room. A quick peek out the peephole revealed Mike's and Donna's smiling faces.

He threw open the door. "Come on in, you guys. I was just about to serve champagne and caviar."

"Jeez," Donna said, wide-eyed. "This is some place. You got it made, Casey."

"I'd just as soon be at home."

"Oh, me, too," the woman retorted. "My place used to look just like this. I just decided to cover the

Italian marble with good old vinyl. It helps me fit in with the neighbors, you know.''

''What's she doing here?'' Brooks asked Mike, who had closed the door and was now studying the ornate gilded frame of the mirror near the door.

''She wanted to see the joint.''

''I thought Dixon didn't want anybody to know where I was.''

''I'm not just anybody,'' Donna said, grinning as she stepped down from the raised entryway and onto the elegant pale peach carpeting in the expansive main room. ''And you know partners share everything.''

Stowing his gun in a holster draped over a chair, Brooks followed her and Mike to the grouping of tan leather sofas in front of the marble fireplace.

''I thought you might be lonely,'' Mike said.

''For you two?''

Donna sank down on the luxurious couch with an appreciative sigh. ''My, but we are testy, aren't we?''

Brooks took a deep breath. ''I'm sorry. I guess I am getting a little stir-crazy up here. But this is Thursday, and I've been up here a while. What's going on in the real world?''

''Aren't you going to ask about Holly and Zane first?'' Mike asked. ''That's been the first question every other time I've come to visit.''

Brooks cut his eyes toward Donna, who was grinning to beat the band. ''Partners share everything, huh?''

''He didn't have to tell me.'' Donna rolled her eyes. ''I knew you were gone on her from the beginning.''

''I'm not gone—''

"Please," Mike cut in. "Could we not argue about this? Frankly, Brooks, I don't care how you choose to represent your feelings for Holly. But she's fine. And by the way, your folks are doing good, too. Me and Donna paid them a visit last night, just to reassure them."

"How about Zane?"

Grinning, Mike dug a roll of Lifesaver candies out of the pocket of his coat. "That boy's something else."

"What does that mean?"

Mike popped one of the candies in his mouth, still grinning. "Just that he's a neat kid."

"I know."

"He sent you a surprise," Donna added, exchanging another smile with Mike.

Brooks frowned at them, not sure what was up. "Let's have it."

"Sure." Mike strode toward the door, threw it open. *And in walked Holly.*

They had at least attempted to disguise her. Her blue jeans were covered by a big white apron of the sort that a maid at a hotel might wear. And her glorious auburn hair was hidden under a scarf. She was pushing a cart filled with cleaning supplies. And seeing her made Brooks's heart trip into overdrive.

"Surprise," Donna quipped.

Her smile tentative, Holly took a step forward. But Brooks didn't smile back. Instead, he growled, "What in the hell is this?"

"Company," Mike told him, closing the door behind Holly.

"Get her out of here."

His words made Holly's smile freeze, but Brooks didn't pause to worry about that. He was too angry with his fellow detectives. "How could you do this?" he demanded.

"This place is a fortress," Donna protested, getting up from the sofa. "Every possible entrance and exit is secured."

"But what if Dante knows I'm in here?"

"How would he know that?" Mike demanded.

"You could have been followed."

Mike's pudgy features turned florid. "You think I wasn't careful? You think I would take a chance like that?"

Brooks hesitated. "Not intentionally."

"You're damn straight about that," Donna cut in. "You're not the only hotshot on the force that knows what he's doing, you know. We were careful, Brooks. We cleared the whole thing with Dixon, too."

"We actually thought you might be glad to see Holly," Mike added.

For the first time, Holly spoke. Eyes narrowed, voice tense, she said, "Obviously all of us made one big mistake. Brooks clearly doesn't want to see me." She turned to the door. "So I'll go."

He caught her arm just as she was about to turn the doorknob. His anger barely controlled, he made her face him. "Holly, I'm not trying to hurt you."

She jerked away. "Gee, I'd hate to see how it goes when you really do try."

"It's just not safe for you to be here."

Defiance burned in her gaze. "Safe for whom? Me? Or is it yourself you're trying to protect?"

The truth of that statement knocked him back a step.

"Tell me," she pressed, moving closer to him. "Tell me what you're so afraid of."

He found his voice at last. "I'm afraid you'll be hurt."

"Isn't that a chance I have a right to take?"

"Holly—"

"Why do you get to make all the choices? Don't I have a vote about us?"

"Us?"

She lifted her chin another notch. "There is an 'us,' isn't there? Saturday night, there was. Saturday night, we were—"

From somewhere behind them, a throat was cleared. Brooks turned, almost surprised to see anyone else in the room.

"I've got a suggestion," Donna offered. "Why don't Mike and I leave? We'll check back in an hour or so, and if Holly wants to go home then, we'll come get her."

Mike nodded. "Or she can stay as long as she wants."

"She should go now," Brooks said, though not with quite as much force as he had displayed earlier.

"No," she said firmly. Stepping away from Brooks, she took off the scarf that covered her head and walked down to the living area. A pull or two at the pins holding her hair in the bun at her nape set the silky auburn waves free to bounce to her shoulders. She pulled off the voluminous apron, as well, and stood silhouetted, tall and curvy and alluring, against the fading early winter sunlight.

And against his will, Brooks felt arousal spiral through him.

"We'll see you later, big guy." Donna paused by Brooks's side, raised on tiptoes and brushed an unexpected kiss across his cheek. "Be cool," she whispered. "I really like her."

Mike clapped him on the shoulder and followed Donna.

"Thanks, guys," Holly called before the two detectives went out. "I'll see you in the *morning*."

Brooks didn't miss the emphasis she put on the last word. As the door closed behind Mike and Donna, he thrust his hands in the pockets of his jeans. "The morning?"

"I told Nana Flora and Zane not to expect me until tomorrow. That I was coming to see you."

"But, Holly—"

She took a step forward. "Don't you want to see me, Brooks? Don't you want me?"

Coming down into the living area toward her, he raked a hand through his hair. "That's not the issue. It's not safe."

"But I feel safe."

"That's not the point."

"But it is," she replied, stepping in front of him. "Don't you remember? I told you that night at the pizza parlor that I didn't feel safe at all, that I felt like I was tightroping over a pit."

"And I was the alligator waiting below."

She slipped her arms around his waist, grinning up at him. "I've decided I like alligators."

Her lips were too sweet, too temptingly near for Brooks to resist. Groaning in submission, he claimed her mouth with his. She melted against him, all warm and curved and welcoming. He knew he was weak. He knew she didn't belong here, that she didn't belong with him anywhere.

Those thoughts made him break away with a protest. "Holly, I don't want to mislead you. I'm not sure—"

She silenced him with another kiss, then drew back, a reckless gleam in her dark eyes. "Tonight, all I'm asking for is this."

"But later—"

"Shh." She kissed him with all the power and need and passion he could ever have dreamed of.

Her hands went to the buckle of his belt and pulled it open.

And a sound, half chuckle, half moan escaped his lips. "In a hurry, aren't you?"

"I'm afraid you may try to throw me out of here in an hour." Still grinning, she unsnapped his jeans and drew the zipper downward. Slowly, carefully, enticingly. Then her hand slipped inside, cupping him, and Brooks felt his last bit of resistance crumble.

Sighing, he said, "You're awfully persuasive, Miss MacPherson."

"Thanks." Through his briefs, she stroked his stiffening, growing need. "And I think you're awfully *ready,* Lieutenant Casey."

He stilled her hand, lifted it away. "Not so fast."

Her smile flashed again as she moved back. "Why?" Keeping her gaze leveled on his, she began unbuttoning the simple cotton shirt she wore.

Brooks followed her movements with hungry eyes. "Don't you think we should at least find a bed?"

"Do we need a bed?" She slipped the blouse from her shoulders, revealing a white silky undergarment. Her skin was creamy perfection against the fragile lace trim. And through the thin material, her breasts were clearly visible, the dusky circles of her nipples hardening in the center.

Inhaling sharply, Brooks brought his hands to her breasts just as she dropped her blouse to the floor. Holly sighed her pleasure as he touched her, lifting her chin to expose the long, beautiful line of her throat. Mesmerized by the beauty she offered, he brushed his thumbs across the tiny peaks that jutted so enticingly forward beneath his hands.

"Maybe we don't need a bed," he murmured, bending down to press his lips against the pulse in her throat.

"That couch looks awfully comfortable to me."

But she deserved a bed, he thought. A wide, comfortable bed with sheets like silk, a bed where he could stretch her out, touch her, make her ache for him. A bed like the luxurious one he had been tossing and turning in alone for the past five nights.

Decision made, he took her by the hand and drew her across the plush carpet toward the bedroom. "We don't have to settle for a sofa when there's a bed like this waiting."

He threw open the carved mahogany doors at the end of the room, revealing polished wooden floors covered with Oriental rugs and heavy, brass-fitted furniture. In the center of the room sat the bed—a vast sea of rumpled cream sheets rising from a golden spread pooled on the floor.

"That's some bed," Holly murmured.

"Try it out." Brooks stepped to the side with a sweeping gesture. "See how it feels."

"All right." A teasing smile on her face, Holly kicked off her loafers, then crossed the room and slipped onto the bed, shimmying backward with movements guaranteed to drive a man to madness. Once she was in the center, she turned on her side, facing him. Her bright hair and shining features were vivid against the sheets, the lines of her body a study in temptation, and her voice was a husky entreaty as she patted the sheets beside her. "Care to join me?"

Shedding his shirt and shoes, Brooks complied. Holly moved into his arms without hesitation, meeting his kiss, fitting her form to his. When his hands pulled down the straps of her lacy underwear, she drew away, sitting up and boldly drawing the garment over her head. Her breasts swung forward, heavy but firm, paler than the skin of her shoulders and arms. Propping himself up on his elbow, Brooks skimmed gentle fingers over her delicate, beautiful flesh. Holly shivered, and for the first time since she had announced her intention to stay here, Brooks saw uncertainty in her expression.

Lying back, he drew her with him, whispering quiet words of reassurance, tucking her head against his shoulder. His fingers tangled in her soft, thick hair. "It's okay. We'll take it slow, Holly. We can take it as slow as you want."

"But that's not what I want," she said. "I want you so much, Brooks. Now." She drew in a shuddering breath. "But it's been so long. And it's never been . . . like this."

"Not for me, either." The admission slipped out. Words Brooks had never said to another woman. He compounded them with "I've never felt like this at all."

Pleased beyond measure, Holly let her fingers slide over his broad chest, through the furring of hair in the center. His muscles were sturdy and well-defined to her touch. His skin was warm, and scented with an elusive male musk. She dipped her head, tasting him with her lips and then her tongue, gliding across taut male nipples and smooth, golden skin. But that didn't last, because he brought her face back up to his, kissing her deeply, soulfully, in a way she was certain only Brooks could ever kiss her.

Their embrace ended with his groan of frustration. "I'm going to explode," he told her bluntly. "Any minute."

But rather than increasing the trepidation she had been feeling only moments before, his explicit admission sent excitement streaming over her. Her hand drifted back to the bulge so clearly outlined beneath his open zipper and white briefs. But he caught her hand before she touched him again.

"If you have any mercy, don't. Let's just cool it a minute. Take a breath. Let me—"

"No."

Quickly, she edged off the bed and, with her back to Brooks, stripped out of her jeans and panties. For just a moment, she fought a new case of insecurity, but then Brooks was beside her, his clothes disposed of, as well. He turned her around, kissed her before she could give in to her nerves. Naked, his body felt even broader, stronger than ever. He was the living embodiment of hard, male power, from his chest, to his arms and legs, to the heaviness of his arousal pressed low against her belly.

And yet that power was laced with tenderness as he kissed her, as he suckled at her breasts, as his touch threaded through the tangle of curls guarding her dewy, feminine cleft. He laid her back on the bed with infinite care, parted her legs with the same restraint. Muscles quivering, he raised himself over her, pausing just as she felt the velvety, hot tip of hardness between her thighs.

"Holly," he whispered. "Sweet Holly."

Pressing her hand down between their bodies, she guided him inside, lifted her hips, accepted his long, exquisite plunge.

Poetry. That was the only word that described how she felt as he danced inside her. Like the perfect blend of meter and verse, rhythm and rhyme, his movements were artful pleasure. She had waited so long for this moment, waited for the pain of betrayal to fade, waited for a man she could trust.

And Brooks didn't disappoint her. He pulled her with him, each thrust carrying her deeper into a boundless bliss. The rapture built as she wrapped herself around him, tightened and moved and arched her body, until Brooks emptied himself into her, until she joined him on the edge and then fell.

Spinning down from the heights in his arms, she called out his name, shamelessly protesting when he would have withdrawn from her. But she couldn't let him go. Sated beyond every expectation she had ever had, she didn't want to lose the joy of these sensations. Like so many shooting stars, her emotions seemed to light her up from the inside.

Brooks complied with Holly's need, carrying her with him as he reversed their positions. He absorbed her light weight as they lay immobile on the tangled, damp sheets. Long, silent moments passed while nightfall painted the room in shadows. The gold-flecked walls turned to deep ocher, and the corners to rich purple. Slow, sweet minutes unwound as his passion played out its final thrumming vibration, as Holly's heart beat hard against his.

Then she moved, stretching her body, as sexy and sinuous as a ballet dancer. Hands flat against his chest, she pushed herself up, straddling his hips. His arousal came back, and the union of their bodies, never really broken, was complete once more.

She pushed down, moving her hips in a lazy circle. As if in a dream, he followed her lead. Slow and then fast, then slower again, like a spring rainstorm dodging the sunshine. Their movements carried them up, pushed them over.

Sprawling across him, Holly slipped into an effortless slumber. But the room, the world, whirled around Brooks. Rocked and twirled and refused to still. He wondered if equilibrium would ever be his again. He was still wondering when exhaustion finally pulled him into sleep.

Chapter Nine

"Champagne?"

Through a haze of steam, Brooks watched Holly pause in the bathroom doorway. She held a champagne bottle in one hand, two glasses in the other. But his interest centered on the filmy lace nightgown she wore. "Where'd you get the gown?"

"Same place as the champagne," she explained, grinning as she crossed the marble floor and approached the whirlpool where he was soaking. The creamy skin of her long legs flashed in and out of revealing side slits. "I packed everything I thought we'd need for the night in that cleaning cart Mike made me bring up the elevator."

"What made you think you'd need a lace nightgown?"

"Just a foolish notion I had."

Lazily, he pushed himself to a sitting position. "You look good."

"You think so?" With a saucy smile, she bent to place the already opened bottle and the glasses on the side of the tub. The plunging lace neckline pulled away from her breasts, providing Brooks with an altogether fascinating view.

"Real good," he murmured, letting his gaze rove over her. Incredibly, desire curled in his belly just as if they hadn't made love twice only a couple of hours before. But there was one thing he didn't understand. "I'm a little surprised at you."

Holly straightened. "What do you mean?"

"That's just not the sort of nightgown a chaste single mother keeps on hand."

"Maybe I was hoping I wouldn't be chaste forever."

"And you were right."

"Definitely." Leaning over the shallow marble steps that led up to the tub, she kissed him. But when he reached to pull her closer, she backed away. "Just wait." She gave a flirtatious sway of her hips and disappeared out the door again, despite Brooks's protests.

She came back carrying a tray filled with bread, cheese and fruit, which she placed beside the champagne. "I found all this in the kitchen. I hope it doesn't belong to whomever owns the apartment."

"Dixon had the place stocked for me. He said to make myself at home, but not to destroy anything. Repairs to this place might be a little out of the department's budget."

"I guess replacing a few candles wouldn't be too difficult." She indicated the clusters of fat white candles arranged at various angles around the tub.

"Sure."

"Good. I found some matches in the kitchen, too." Quickly, she lit the candles, then switched out all the lights except those that glowed beneath the surface of the water.

"Nice," Brooks murmured, watching her move toward the tub again. She deftly scooped her hair back and secured it up in a twist. The white gown swirled around her, diaphanous and alluring, blurring the outline of her womanly shape. The color was as innocent as the style wasn't. And the sight of her was driving him crazy. "Aren't you coming in?"

"Of course." Lithely, she pulled the gown over her head, and it fluttered to floor like a pair of discarded angel's wings. Brooks grinned at the image. For it was vixen instead of angel that he wanted to share this tub with.

She mounted the steps with the grace of a queen, then stepped in and settled next to him with a contented sigh. The candlelight reflected in her shining hair and dark eyes, while outside the ten-foot window over the tub, the city gleamed like their own personal postcard.

Brooks poured champagne and handed her a glass, laughing when she wrinkled her nose over the bubbles. "This is the life, don't you think?"

"It's nice," she admitted.

"Nice?" He nodded toward the window. "Just that view alone is worth millions."

"I suppose I could endure it at least a couple of times a year."

"Only a couple?"

"I like the view at home, too."

"Opulence looks awfully good on you."

She shrugged, her shoulders rising out of the warm, frothing water. "I've never wanted opulence."

He knew that, of course. He had known from the beginning that all Holly wanted was security, *commitment*. Maybe that knowledge was the imp that prompted Brooks to add, "Good old Joel could have given you a taste of it, more than a few times a year." He hated the pang that gave him.

But Holly's smile remained gentle, luminous. "There were other things he couldn't give me."

"Come here." Setting his glass on the side of the tub, Brooks opened his arms to her.

She went into them, putting her head against his chest, seemingly as content as a woman with a world of riches. He dropped a kiss against her hair, inhaling her fragrance, savoring the weight of her body against his.

But there was something he needed to get out of the way before he became completely turned on again. "I need to apologize to you, Holly."

She drew back. "For what?"

He cleared his throat, feeling like an idiot. "For not taking care of you." When she continued to frown in confusion, he added, "Not using a condom."

Her mouth formed a silent "Oh." Then she said. "It's okay."

"No, it's not."

"But I took care of things."

"How?"

"I take birth control."

He blinked in surprise. "You do?"

"Yes, I do," she replied, sounding defensive.

"How long?"

"A while. I can assure you I'm safe." A line appeared between her eyebrows, and she moved farther away from him. "Anything else you want to know?"

"But why—"

"Because I was hoping there was a night like this in my future."

He was silent for a moment, taking that in. Then realization hit. "You started on the pill when you were dating Joel."

Her wide-eyed look was all the answer he needed.

Standing abruptly, he sloshed water onto the sides of the tub, dousing several of the candles.

"Oh, that's nice," Holly said. "Just get all macho and mad about a man I never once desired, that I never did more than kiss."

Knowing he was being unreasonable but not caring, Brooks grabbed a towel from the stack beside the tub, stepped out and wrapped it around his middle.

"All I did was consider sleeping with him," Holly continued. "And after having been left alone one time after getting pregnant, I wasn't about to go through it again. A long time ago, I made up my mind to never trust another man with birth control."

Because she hadn't been able to trust him, either, Brooks paused on the bottom step from the tub. His indignation over Joel fled like so much hot air.

"So don't be getting all jealous about something I did for my own sake. You ought to be grateful that I'm safe. You certainly didn't give the matter any thought until after the fact."

The truth stung. Shamefaced, Brooks did a slow turn back to face her. "I guess I'm a jerk."

"A macho jerk," Holly snapped.

"Whatever you say."

"Like most cops."

That was a surprise. "What do you mean by that?"

"Just what I said."

"But your grandfather...I mean, the way I've heard you talk about him, he was a great guy."

"He was terrific. He'd have died for me or Nana or Zane. But he was also pigheaded and stubborn and overprotective and he took risks he didn't need to take. And those are only a few of the reasons I used to swear I'd never get involved with a cop. But here I go—doing it again." Getting to her feet, she jerked a towel free from the stack for herself.

Brooks stared at her, confused. "What did you say?"

"You heard me," she muttered, holding the towel in front of her.

"I thought you said, 'Here I go—*again.*'"

Her laugh was short and mirthless. "Didn't Nana Flora tell you?"

"What?"

"Zane's father was a cop."

"What?" he repeated, thunderstruck.

"Don't look so shocked, Brooks."

"He left you."

She laughed at his unnecessary comment. "You don't think a cop could do that? Surely you don't have blinders on."

Brooks shook his head. "Of course not. I know a cop could do that. Cops do rotten things every day, all day. I just…" He bit his lip. "Is it someone still on the force?"

"Are you kidding? That was part of the problem. He didn't want to stay here in Memphis. He was ready to leave the minute I told him the news. He skipped town without giving notice."

"Good thing, probably," Brooks muttered.

"Why do you say that?"

"Because I imagine your grandfather was planning to beat the living hell out of him."

Shoulders slumping, Holly sat down on the edge of the tub, one hand clutching the towel to her breasts. "I imagine he would have. Especially since Papa Jake brought him home to meet me."

"Who was he?"

"Some rookie Papa Jake had taken under his wing. He was just twenty-two, and I was eighteen." She gave a bitter laugh. "And nature took its course."

"But your grandfather felt responsible."

"Of course he did. That's how he was." She sighed, looking suddenly very vulnerable. "But it was no one's fault but mine."

"And the guy's."

"Mine," she insisted. "I wasn't stupid. I should have been careful."

Brooks hated seeing her so hard on herself. "You were young, Holly. You just made a mistake."

"A baby isn't a mistake. People shouldn't say that. Babies aren't mistakes or accidents or just 'oops but I forgot to bring the condom' slipups. They're real, live people, not mistakes. And I should have known that.

That's what I was in the end to my own mother, so I, of all people, shouldn't have been so careless."

"Stop beating yourself up." Having heard all he could, Brooks climbed the steps, came around the tub and sat down next to Holly, letting his feet trail in the bubbling water. "I bet for everything that you did wrong, you've done penance a thousand times over."

"Penance for not using birth control is three-o'clock feedings and the terrible twos," she said wryly.

Relieved to see her good humor reappear, he was reluctant to get serious again. Yet he had to. "I'm sorry," he said, gently touching her cheek. "I'm sorry I didn't protect you. And I'm sorry I got so hot over Joel. But the thought, just the *thought,* of you with someone else did something crazy to my brain."

"That's so dumb."

"And so male. We're all just big lugs, you know."

The faintest glimmer of a smile appeared on her lips.

"I see that," Brooks teased. "And I know that secretly, somewhere down in that liberated heart of yours, you like knowing there are men who would fight for you, who can't stand the thought of sharing you."

Her smile deepened, though she protested, "That's barbaric."

"It's natural. No matter how the lines blur between what men and women do, there are still some as-signed roles."

She arched one skeptical eyebrow. "What's my role when I'm fighting with a patient in E.R.?"

"That's where everything blurs."

"But what if someone came through that door right now, threatening us, and it was me who had the chance to save you?"

"You'd do it," Brooks admitted.

"So everything blurs again."

Chuckling, he shook his head. "I can't win with you, can I?"

She ducked her head, looking up at him through a fan of black, silky lashes as she let her towel drop. "I think you have won, Brooks."

He felt distinctly triumphant as he cast his own towel aside and slipped back into the heated, foaming water. Wrapping his arms around her legs, he pulled her down with him. She fit easily against the curved marble, and his body fit easily to hers. But instead of kissing her, or touching her and starting the spiral of desire that he knew could follow, he said, "Tell me about Papa Jake."

"I thought I had."

He shook his head. "Until tonight, I thought he was some sort of minor deity. This is the first I've heard that he might have failings."

"He was a man."

"And a bit of a legend on the force, from what Mike has told me."

Her smile was tender. "People used to say that sometimes, but Papa Jake always laughed. He said he was just a beat cop."

"Why didn't he move up past sergeant?"

"He didn't want to. He had worked in the same sector of the city for a long time. He said he liked being part of the neighborhood." She looked away. "Only it was one of the Memphis neighborhoods that's not so great anymore. And it got him in the end.''

''What happened?''

''He was trying to break up a fight,'' she said, so offhandedly that Brooks knew she was hiding her pain. ''Some kid jumped him from behind, another hit him in front. His ribs were broken. He had a concussion. His back was damaged. His knees were already a mess, but this scuffle blew them out completely. He had to have physical therapy just to walk. And from then on, it was one ailment after another. He never completely recovered.''

''He died from those injuries?'' The story sounded somewhat familiar to Brooks, but he had a hard time believing he wouldn't have remembered a cop who died after being beaten by a group of punks.

''Pneumonia.'' Her eyes filled with tears, which she tried to blink away. ''People aren't supposed to die of pneumonia anymore. But he did. One night, when we thought he was doing okay, he just slipped away.''

Brooks held her, absorbing her silent sobs. Her tears never overflowed. She held them in with a control he both admired and regretted. He had a feeling she should cry.

''I think,'' he whispered, ''that I would have liked your Papa Jake.''

''Probably,'' she admitted. Then bitterness claimed her features again. ''You could have if he had just walked away from that fight.''

''You know he couldn't.''

''It was a couple of gang bangers that are probably dead by now.''

"I know from experience he didn't even think about that. His training just kicked in, Holly."

"I wish it hadn't. I wish he had thought about Nana and me and Zane before he waded in, trying to do his good deed."

"It was his job."

Her expression filled with anguish, she said, "But why did it have to be him?"

"There's no answer for that."

"I know, but—" With a cry that seemed to come straight from her soul, she turned, wrapping her arms around Brooks and letting go of her tears. Like a dam under too much pressure for far too long, she just cracked. She cried so hard that he ached for her. But when the storm was through, he also felt her relief. He was left to wonder if she had ever cried for her grandfather.

"Hold me," she said, her voice still choked with tears.

He gripped her tightly. "Of course."

"And love me. Love me now."

Instinctively, he accepted the lips she raised to his, accepted the urgency of her embrace, accepted the passion she offered.

He took her swiftly, against the side of the tub. It was exactly as Holly wanted it. Hard and fast. Powerful enough to erase the lingering sadness that thinking of her grandfather had brought. Potent enough to chase away her tears.

She needed Brooks to fill her, to overwhelm her senses, to stop the fear that was creeping in around the edges of this night she had claimed as her own with him.

Fear, because there was a madman who might want him dead.

Fear, because even when that was done, he would still be a cop. Always and forever a cop.

Fear, because she loved him in spite of everything else she knew.

After years of rising before the sun, Holly's internal alarm clock wasn't easy to turn off. She came awake Friday morning while it was still dark. And she knew instantly where she was. Of course, since Brooks was holding her, spoon fashion, in his arms, there was no chance for the disorientation that might be experienced when a person awoke in a strange room.

"Do you always wake up like that?" he whispered against her ear.

"How do you mean?"

"With a little jump."

"I wouldn't know, and since I don't usually wake up with someone else, no one's ever told me so."

"Then I guess I'll have to find out."

Smiling into the darkness, she said, "Does that mean you've changed your mind and I can stay another night?"

He went completely still. "No."

She released a long, disappointed breath, but she didn't press. They'd had this argument last night. And despite all her cajoling, even her blatant attempts at sexual bribery, he had remained firm. He had called Mike before midnight to tell him to be here this morning at nine to get her.

"I'm not going to stay here much longer myself," he murmured now.

Her hand tightened on the arm he had draped across her waist. "What do you mean?"

"I'm tired of sitting up here, waiting. If Dixon thinks I'm not really a target, then I'm just wasting time."

He had told her last night about the theory that Dixon had about Dante's real intentions. Holly could see that it made sense. Yet she also appreciated the captain's caution in stowing Brooks away for a while. "But what if he's wrong, and you are a target?"

He hugged her back against him. "I can take care of myself, Holly."

"How?"

"By staying alert."

"I wish I thought that was enough."

"It's a good cop's best weapon."

The word *weapon* made her squeeze her eyes shut.

"Don't worry," Brooks soothed. As if to underscore his words, he stroked one broad, strong hand up her side, from thigh to her breast. There his fingers curved, moving lightly over the instantly pebbled nipple.

"You can distract me all you want," she told him. "But that won't make me stop worrying."

"All right." Pushing himself up on his elbow, he pressed a series of lingering kisses to her shoulder. His touch on her breast grew more deliberate. And against her lower back, she felt him stir.

"That's nice," she whispered. "A very nice distraction."

"Well, I'm glad you approve. I like being nice." His voice was a deep rumble as he took his hand from her breast, pushing it down between their bodies, over the curves of her bottom. Without hesitation, she parted her legs, and his fingers slipped gently forward between her thighs. After last night, she was tender here, and he seemed to know that. His touch was so delicate, so light, yet so perfectly on target. After only a moment or so, she was rotating her hips toward the pressure of his hand.

She murmured a mindless protest when he withdrew that circling, arousing touch. She barely had time to realize what he was doing before he pushed her legs farther apart, shifted his own body, then filled her slick, feminine folds. She gasped at his hard length, at the sheer eroticism of their position. Then gasped again as he began to move.

Her completion came almost immediately. In hard, driving waves. He took much longer, and so she rode the crest again and again, until he poured into her.

Even after last night, Holly had never imagined anything like this splintering sensation. She was lost, she realized, totally lost. She didn't know if she'd survive without this man. So that meant he had to survive and come back to her.

Turning in his arms with a little sob, she held him as tightly as humanly possible. He seemed to know without words what she was thinking.

"I'll be okay," he murmured. "I promise I'll be okay."

She nodded, not trusting herself to speak.

Several minutes passed before Brooks spoke again. "I have a confession to make. It's about something you said yesterday. You said that maybe I wanted you to leave, not to protect you, but because I was protecting myself."

She nodded, silently waiting for him to continue.

"You were right," he said after a pause.

"But what are you afraid of?"

"Of feeling something for you."

"Why is that so bad?"

He took a deep breath, exhaled, then shook his head. "It's complicated, Holly. I'm not even sure I've got it sorted out in my head. But I do know this. For me, relationships have always been about the chase."

"The chase?"

"Getting the girl." He chuckled softly. "At about this time in any of my previous entanglements, I would already be thinking of a way out."

She swallowed hard. "And now?"

"Now, I keep thinking of the next time. The next time I'll see you, kiss you, laugh with you. And that doesn't even begin to cover all the other things I keep thinking we might do."

Snuggling against his chest, she said, "So what does this mean?"

"I don't know."

It wasn't the answer she had wanted. "What do you think?"

"I'm not sure."

She didn't like that answer, either. But Holly knew, deep down, that she wasn't likely to get a declaration of undying love from Brooks. At least not yet. So she stopped pushing.

They managed to get out of bed a little while later, shared a simple breakfast, bathed and dressed and then stood together looking out at the view of the city coming to life under overcast December skies. And at nine on the dot, when the doorbell chimed, Holly was afraid she couldn't go. She feared she was going to make a big, emotional scene.

But she turned out to be stronger than that. She was proud of the way she hugged Brooks and said good-bye and rode down the elevator with Mike and Donna.

At home, Nana Flora waited. With her wise eyes, she no doubt saw exactly what had transpired between Holly and Brooks. If her smile was any indication, she approved.

Holly kept herself busy all day, even calling her supervisor to say she was available for duty if they needed her. And, of course, they needed her that night. Holly wanted to be busy, too busy to think about what Brooks might be doing, too busy to wonder about what would happen when all this was resolved.

She waited to leave for the hospital, however, until Zane was home. He got off the bus, ran across the yard and front porch, full of excitement, calling her name. She met him in the foyer.

"Did you see Brooks?" he demanded.

"Yeah." She squeezed his shoulder. "I owe you one for getting Mike to smuggle me in."

"That's okay," Zane replied with a cheeky grin. "Is Brooks okay?"

"He's just fine."

"When can I see him?"

"Soon."

"Aw, Mom. That's not an answer."

Capturing his chin in her palm, she tilted his bright little face upward. "It's the only answer I've got, big guy."

A new glimmer of maturity won out over childish impatience. He nodded, then eyed her with interest. "So you're going to work?"

"What can I say? They can't do without me for another day."

His smile split his face.

"What's this? Are you glad I'm not going to be home tonight?"

"Nah. It's just normal, you know, you going to work."

She didn't have time to try to puzzle the workings of his young mind. Brushing a kiss across his forehead and calling a goodbye to Nana Flora, she left for the hospital.

While her car backed out of the drive, Zane stood waving on the porch. He felt as if a rock had been lifted off his chest. Mom was going to work. And she was smiling. *Really* smiling. Finally, things were going right again.

Chapter Ten

Typical for a Friday night, the E.R. was hopping. By nine, they had already seen the victims of two stabbings and several car accidents, as well as the usual coughs, cuts and stomach complaints. Holly was almost relieved to be assigned to clean the wounds of a man who had fallen off his roof while trying to replace some burned-out Christmas lights.

"Those damn prickly pear bushes broke my fall," he muttered, wincing as she swabbed one of his many lacerations with disinfectant.

She stepped close, examining a nasty-looking cut on his cheek and making a notation on the chart for the doctor. "On the other hand, you might have really been injured if the bushes hadn't been there."

He grimaced up at her. "You must be an optimist."

"Let's just say I'm an optimist tonight. Now, to-morrow, if the lights on my roof go out..."

Holly and the patient were sharing a laugh when someone called her name from the doorway of the treatment cubicle.

"Yes," she answered.

"Holly."

With an impatient sigh, she turned to find Mrs. Coulter and another nurse standing in the doorway. They both looked kind of strange. "What is it?" Holly asked.

"Let Marge take over here," Mrs. Coulter said.

"Why?"

"Because I need you in another room."

A dull roar started in Holly's ears as she handed the medication to the other nurse. There was something in Mrs. Coulter's face...

"What is it?" she demanded the minute they were out of the cubicle. "What's wrong? Zane?"

"No." Mrs. Coulter took her arm as they pushed through the double doors that led from that treatment area to a smaller area they called Trauma One Receiving. The first thing Holly saw was Donna's face. Donna was in one corner of the room and puffing in another door was Captain Dixon. Because Holly saw them first, she was ready when the swarm of people parted around the gurney in the center of the room.

She was ready to see Brooks.

Suddenly numb, she shrank against the wall, out of the way of everyone working to help Brooks. A bullet, she heard, had entered one side of his neck, exiting through the back of his shoulder. Another had caught his thigh. His vitals were weak, he had lost a lot of blood, and they were prepping him for immediate surgery.

At her side, Mrs. Coulter said, "Are you okay, Holly?"

"Yes."

The older woman, normally so stern, squeezed her hand. "You just hold on. He'll need to see you smiling when he comes out of this." Then she bustled off.

Through the windows that separated this trauma room from others, Holly could see there were other patients arriving. This was big, she thought, trembling, as big as Brooks said it might be.

Mrs. Coulter had said *when,* not *if* he came out of this. Holly grabbed hold of those words, trying to use them to stop the hope that was seeping out of her. Her foolish hopes, inflated by last night with Brooks, buoyed by his admission that he'd never felt for another woman as he did for her. Stupid, stupid hopes. They were no good to her now.

Holly stayed against the wall, not moving toward the other policemen until Brooks was pushed out of the trauma room to surgery. Then she faced them with anger. "What in the hell happened?"

Donna took her arm. "Everything went down tonight. Dante drew a line in the sand, and it was on someone else's turf, someone who decided to shoot it out. We got tipped, so we were on the scene, too."

"But why was Brooks there?" Holly wheeled to Captain Dixon. "Why did you let him be there?"

"He was needed," the big man explained. "He wanted to be there, and we needed him on the scene. I decided the decision was his."

"And now he's shot. Dante got him."

"No," Donna said, turning Holly to face her. "It wasn't that way. This wasn't a hit. Bullets were flying everywhere." She gestured toward the next gurney the EMT's were wheeling into position. "We've got all kinds of people down. Mike's heading up the team at the scene, trying to sort it all out."

"Other officers are down?"

"No," Dixon admitted. "Just Brooks."

"And what about Dante?"

The two cops traded looks, but Dixon spoke, "As far as we can tell, he was nowhere near the place."

"Of course." Muttering an oath of despair, Holly stalked away from them, through the doors where Brooks had disappeared. Instead of waiting for an elevator, she raced up the stairs to the surgical floor, all the way into the glassed room outside the operating room.

She couldn't see anything beyond the huddle of green coats surrounding Brooks. But Holly stayed there, hands pressed against the glass until Mrs. Coulter appeared at her side and convinced her to sit down and wait outside.

Brooks's parents were waiting, too, with his sisters Carmen and Mary Jane. Donna had called them. And she and Captain Dixon kept a vigil of their own at the other end of the room.

White-faced, grim, the Casey family cleared a space at their center for Holly. An hour ticked past. The waiting went on. Finally, when Holly knew she was going to scream, the surgeon appeared at the door.

And he said exactly what she had expected. They still had to wait. The next few hours were critical. Brooks was a strong man. The bullet had missed the major arteries and nerves, but there was still extensive damage. All any of them could do was wait. The doctor suggested they all go home, get some rest. There'd be more information in the morning.

But Holly just sat down again. His family joined her. There was no discussion about leaving.

The first thing Brooks heard was Holly's voice. As he swam up out of the sludge that was pulling at his limbs, he heard her. She was saying his name, again and again, urging him to wake up. He did, but he couldn't focus his eyes. Not for several moments, anyway. But when he did, her face filled his vision.

"You're going to be fine," she told him. "Just fine."

"What happened?" His voice was little more than a croak, his mouth so dry he could barely pull his tongue down from the roof.

"You got shot."

"I know that. But what happened?"

"Just go to sleep, Brooks. Go back to sleep."

He did. And when he awoke the next time, he was clearer. His mother's face had joined Holly's. They both stood over him. They both smiled. Then another nurse hurried in, pushing Holly and his mother out of the way. This nurse did so many horrible things to Brooks's body that he tried to drift back off again. The only good thing she did was give him a swallow of water. He wanted to gulp a whole bucketful, but she said no.

Holly said no, as well, when she reappeared and he asked her for water. But she patted his hand and stroked his face, and before he slipped back under the sludge again, she said she loved him.

It was those words that thundered through his brain when he awoke the next time. Brooks felt much, much clearer now. His head ached like hell, but at least he could think. They had him laid almost flat on a bed, and he couldn't lift his head. But if he turned to the right, he could see Holly. Pain stabbed through his neck at the movement. But it wasn't so bad he couldn't stand it. He turned and stared at Holly, asleep in the chair beside his bed.

Weak sunlight threaded through the institutional blinds and fell across her face. She was pale, drawn looking. And her uniform was a wrinkled mess. Brooks had to wonder how long she had been here.

Closing his eyes, he turned away from her again. He couldn't stand seeing her looking that way, knowing he was the reason. She reminded him of Markowitz's wife on the night Dan had been beaten. Brooks had sat beside Kendra Markowitz, aware of her pain and resolving never to put anyone through that. And yet what had he done? He hadn't been strong enough to push Holly away. He had let their relationship develop. And now she was in love with him. His own feelings for her were of no consequence. He refused to even put a name to them. All that mattered was Holly thought she loved him. And that love could only bring her sorrow.

Never get involved with a cop.

She had said it herself. She knew what she had done. But Brooks knew she wouldn't back away now on her own. Somehow, when he was stronger, he had to push her away.

That resolve was the last thing he thought of before he drifted off once more.

Nearly sixty hours after Brooks had been brought in, Holly was finally persuaded to leave the hospital. She went home, slept for ten hours straight, assured Zane and Nana that Brooks was fine, then went back to see him.

His mother was coming out of his room as Holly approached. Regina greeted her with a smile. "He's almost his old self this morning. Grouchy and fretting about being in bed. The doctors are pleased with his progress."

"Astounded is more like it."

"Well, I'm off to work," Regina said, backing away. "If all goes well, Brooks should be out of here in a few days. I hope you and Zane and your grandmother will come with him to Christmas Eve dinner at our house. I think it's time our families got together."

"I think that can be arranged," Holly agreed. She was smiling as she pushed open the door.

Brooks was sitting up in bed. His neck and shoulder were still swathed in bandages, but his color was good. Someone had shaved him this morning and washed his hair, and he did look almost like his old self. Except for the grim look on his face.

"What's wrong?" Holly asked, her smile fading.

He shook his head.

"I guess you're just tired of being in this bed. Have they gotten you up and walking?"

"Last night."

"Then you'll be feeling better soon." Crossing the room, Holly set a basket of cookies from Nana Flora on the table beside his bed. Then she reached to open the blinds a little wider.

"Leave them," Brooks said shortly.

She looked at him in concern. "Are you okay?"

"Right as rain."

The sarcasm knocked her back a step. But he had been through a lot, so if he were in a bad mood, she could understand. As if he hadn't spoken, she dug in her purse. "I've got a card in here somewhere from Zane. He made it for you himself." Finding the card, she pulled it out and presented it with a flourish. "It's really cute."

Brooks took it, but he didn't open it. Head down, he just turned it over and over in his hands. Holly was beginning to get frightened.

"Brooks, are you sure—"

He looked up at her, his blue eyes, which she knew could be so warm, were as cool and distant as those of a stranger. "I want to talk to you," he said. "About us."

"Us?"

"You, me. Zane." His voice was still gruff.

"What about us?"

"It's no good."

She felt as if he'd slapped her. "No good?"

"Am I not speaking English or something? You keep repeating everything I say."

Dread bloomed in her chest like a deadly weed. "What's wrong with you?"

"Nothing's wrong. In fact, I'm clear as a bell. Clearer than I've been in a while."

"You can't be. You were just shot. You went through traumatic surgery."

"And all of that really cleared up my thinking." He focused those cold, cold eyes on her again. "There's no future for us, Holly."

"You're just saying that because you were hurt, because you don't want me to go through this again."

He closed his eyes, squeezing them shut. "That's not it at all. I mean, haven't you proved you're strong enough to take this? You've been right here all through it. You didn't collapse. You survived right along with me. The chances that I'll ever be hurt again on the job are slim to none if statistics prove anything."

"Then why are you . . ." Swallowing hard, she took a step toward the bed. "Why are you doing this?"

"I just don't love you."

She sucked in her breath. "You don't know that. You told me you didn't know how you felt."

"Well, now I do know."

Scanning his flat, emotionless features, Holly felt desperation push past her fear. "How could you not love me? After the other night—"

"That was about sex."

He might as well have thrown scalding water over her. His words burned her that bad. She felt their sting on her burning skin, inside her skull, and deep, deep in her heart.

And he wasn't through. "The other night was about frustration. Weeks of waiting. Even I have to admit the waiting paid off—very well. But if you had any experience at all, you would realize that sex was all it was. If you were a little more sophisticated, I wouldn't have to tell you."

Somehow, she forced words past the obstruction in her throat. "You . . . bastard."

"I've been called worse."

"How could you do this to me?" Her chest was so tight she was afraid it would burst. "Are you saying you led me on just for sex? You can't tell me that's the only way you can get it. I'm sure there are more willing women—"

"But you made it interesting. I told you I liked the chase, didn't I?"

"And you said a lot more."

"I said what you wanted to hear."

Staring at his handsome features, looking into the face of the man she loved, Holly still couldn't accept what he was saying. "I don't believe you. I don't believe anyone could be that conniving."

"Don't you?" he asked, his mouth twisting in a hard line. "Weren't you fooled before, Holly? By Zane's father?"

She wanted to kill. In that moment, Holly understood the meaning of murder in the heat of passion. Later, she could only be grateful that there wasn't anything nearby that she could really hurt him with. She had to be grateful that her pride kept her from dissolving into one of those weak, spineless creatures that she detested, the kind that begged for love from men who didn't know how to give it.

Turning on her heel, she made for the door, but something occurred to her before she could leave. She spun around to face him again. "What about Zane?" she asked. "What about the boy that wants you for a father? The boy that chose you, brought you home to me, kept bringing us back together? Are you trying to tell me that you used him, his affections, just to get me in the sack? Can you honestly tell me that?''

For a moment, Holly thought she had broken through to the man she knew. A flicker of some emotion—regret?—went across his face as he looked down at the card from Zane that he was still holding. But then he looked up again, his face expressionless, as he crumpled the homemade construction-paper card in his hand. "Yeah," he muttered. "I used him."

She left then. She ran out of the room and down the hall and all the way to her car. Whether he was lying just to drive her away or meant what he had said, she didn't care. He had struck the heart of her insecurities, her fear that she would let a man fool her as Zane's father had. She felt so dirty. So used. All she wanted to do was get home. Home, to the woman who had raised her.

But Zane was there, too, out of school for the Christmas break. She had told him this morning that he could go see Brooks in the hospital today. What could she tell him now? What could she say to that bright, happy little boy? That his mother was a fool, two times over. That she'd been taken in by another man's smooth lies. If she told him that, he would blame himself. She knew her son, knew he often took responsibility for things that weren't his fault. And this time, because he had brought her and Brooks together, he would feel real accountability. She didn't want him to have that burden. But what was she going to tell him?

Fighting for time, she made up a story about Brooks's doctor saying he couldn't have any more visitors until tomorrow. She tried to go about her business as if nothing was wrong. But she knew it was no good. She saw the looks Zane gave her. She knew Nana Flora was studying her.

And that night, when she had paced her floor a thousand times, when she couldn't stand the hurt any longer, she went to Nana. She laid her head in her lap, and the story spilled out. For Holly, there was eerie familiarity in the scene. For hadn't she done the same thing when Zane's father betrayed her? Now, just as then, Nana held her, wiped away her tears, murmured words of comfort that had little impact now, but which Holly knew would soothe her later. She knew the pain would ebb, but right now its sharpness was all too acute.

"What about Zane?" she asked her grandmother. "What am I going to tell him?"

"The truth."

"I can't bear to think of telling him that Brooks used him. I can't. I don't even know how I'd explain the concept of what Brooks was after."

The older woman stroked Holly's hair back from her damp cheeks. "He has to know something. And he has a right to be angry with Brooks."

"I know."

"Talk to him tomorrow, unless..." Nana pursed her lips.

"Unless what?"

"Unless you think Brooks is lying to you, that he really is just pushing you away."

"He was horrible, Nana. The things he said, the way he looked. Why would he do that unless it were true?"

Her wise grandmother had no answer for that.

So the next morning, Holly presented the facts to Zane, at least as many of the facts as she thought he could understand.

He sat quietly, listening to her explanation, then shook his head. "You're wrong. Brooks really cares about us."

"No," Holly said, sitting down beside him. "Brooks has turned out not to be a good person. He let us think he cared about us, but he didn't."

"But why?"

"It's something adults do sometimes. They use people to get what they want."

"But what did he want?"

Holly gathered all her poise and tried to put it simply. "You know the other night, before Brooks got shot, when I went and stayed the night with him?"

"Yeah."

"Well…that's what Brooks wanted. And now that I did that, he's tired of me."

"Tired of you?"

"Yeah. Bored. You know, sort of like you get tired of a toy after a while and you just leave it in your chest."

She must have hit upon just the right analogy, for the anger that grew in Zane's expression was real. "That stinks. How can you let Brooks get away with it? Can't you—"

Holly took hold of his shoulders. "I can't do anything. I don't want to do anything. I'm not going to see him ever again. And you won't, either."

"I wish I'd never brought him here."

Drawing her son tight against her, she murmured, "You can't blame yourself. He fooled me, too. He fooled all of us."

Zane seemed to accept that. But he was quiet the rest of the night, and he went to bed early. Holly didn't blame him. She was so exhausted. All she wanted to do was sleep, sleep deeply enough to erase all that had happened.

"You've got to be kidding." Amazed, Brooks stared up at the man standing over his bed. "Why in the world do I need a guard on my door?"

Dixon shuffled his feet. "Because I was wrong."

"Wrong?"

The captain tossed a plastic bag on the bed. "This came in this afternoon at the precinct."

Brooks picked it up. Inside the bag was a note. "It ain't over, Casey. D.W.," he read, then looked back at Dixon. "Is this some kind of a joke?"

"Apparently not. We took in several of Dante's people after the shooting the other night. Just before this arrived, one of them finally admitted that Dante does want you dead. He was playing with you before, diverting our attention a little. But now that that's blown, now that his operation is pretty much in shambles, this henchman of his figures Dante will really come after you."

Shoving a frustrated hand through his hair, Brooks sat back. "When is this going to end?"

"When we get him, I guess. From all accounts, Dante's gone a little bit mad. The fact that he sent this warning note proves he's not thinking straight."

"Without the note, I'd be taken by surprise. But of course that's not dramatic enough for Dante."

"Exactly," Dixon agreed.

"What are you going to do?"

"Put on guards, then put you back in the penthouse when they release you from here."

Brooks shook his head emphatically. "No way." He never wanted to see that elegant place again. He couldn't stay there, not without remembering Holly spread across that cream-and-gold bed, Holly stepping down into that wide marble tub, Holly in his arms. Holly, Holly, Holly...

"Don't be a fool," Dixon said. "You know it's the perfect place to hide."

"I don't want to hide."

"Now, listen—"

"We played this your way in the beginning," Brooks snapped. "I never wanted to hide. And I won't now. You can take my badge before I'll hide again."

Though his face was grim, Dixon conceded with a sigh, "I guess it should be up to you."

"It *is* my life."

"So you think we just wait."

"For now. And then when I'm out of here, maybe we can make contact, try to set something up with Dante, bait him, pull him in."

"All right." Nodding his head, Dixon stepped away from the bed. "For right now, I'm putting some patrols here in the hospital. Donna and Mike both know what Dante looks like. I'll circulate his picture among the other guards. We'll try to get him when he comes in. And there'll be a guard at your door if he manages to slip by."

"I don't want that guard."

"Casey—"

"If Dante gets in the hospital—which is pretty likely, given all the entrances and exits from this place—and if he sees the guard, he'll either shoot him or just back away. But if he gets in here, I'll be waiting."

"And if you're asleep?"

"I won't be."

Dixon passed a hand over his face. Then he doffed his jacket and unhooked the holster from around his shoulder. "I guess you need a piece, huh?"

"Well, they didn't let me keep mine."

"Take mine," the captain said, offering the gun.

"What about you?"

"I'm not the one Dante wants."

Nodding, Brooks hefted the trim automatic in his hand. It fit his palm well. He only hoped he didn't have to use it.

"Holly, wake up. Now!"

Blinking as the overhead light went on, Holly sat up in bed. Nana Flora stood over her, wringing her hands. "What's wrong?"

"Zane. He's gone."

Instantly wide awake, Holly peered at her clock. It was 4:00 a.m. "Have you looked downstairs?"

"I've looked everywhere. I got up to go to the bathroom, and I saw Wondercat, scratching at Zane's door."

"Wondercat wasn't in with Zane?"

As if he heard his name, the big tom leapt from the floor to Holly's bed and meowed plaintively.

"When I looked in Zane's room, the bed was empty. He stuffed pillows under the covers to look like he was there."

"I thought he was asleep when I looked in before coming to bed," Holly said. "He could have been gone then."

"But where can he be?"

"There's only one possibility, don't you think?"

Nana's eyes widened. "The hospital?"

"Of course." Throwing off the bedcovers, Holly reached for the jeans and sweater she had discarded earlier. Her brave little man had gone off to avenge her honor. Well, he was going to meet an immovable force when he saw Brooks. But then, he'd be lucky if that's all he met up with.

"Call the hospital," she instructed Nana. "Tell the guards to be on the lookout for Zane. I'm heading down there."

Chapter Eleven

Zane was cold, and he was tired and hungry. For as long as he could remember, he had been going to the hospital with his mom, and it always seemed so close. Mom was always saying that was one of the nice things about working there—that it wasn't a long drive. But on his bicycle, in the dark, trying to keep away from places where someone might see him, it was a harder trip. He was just about to give up when he saw the lighted hospital sign up ahead.

In the parking lot, he stowed his bicycle in some bushes, then trudged up the concrete path to the entrance, hiding behind a pillar before going in. There were guards sitting right inside. So there had to be another way.

He skirted around the building toward the emergency entrance, having to dodge a couple of guards along the way. They sure were out tonight. Maybe looking for him.

Zane squared his shoulders at the thought. He doubted his mom or Nana Flora knew he was gone yet. That's why he had set his alarm and put it under his pillow, so he'd get up in time to sneak out and maybe get back back before they knew he was gone. The getting-back part was probably out, since it had taken so long to get here. But he didn't care. He was going to see Brooks.

He had spent a lot of time thinking about what his mom had told him this afternoon about Brooks. Zane just didn't see how it could be true. Brooks was a good guy. Zane had known that about him the minute they met, the minute he called him "little man" and showed him his gun. There was something wrong here. And he was going to straighten it out—man to man— with Brooks. That was the only way a true knight did anything. Man to man.

In the shrubbery near the emergency entrance, Zane crouched down. An ambulance had just pulled up, and they were unloading someone on a stretcher. Everyone was in a hurry, yelling stuff, concentrating on whoever was hurt. And this was Zane's chance.

Ducking his head, he went in the door, straight through to the room where he'd met Brooks and beyond. He kept walking, his head down, trying to look as if he knew what he was doing.

He turned a corner, thinking he was through the hard part, then he saw Lieutenant Mike standing halfway down the hall. Spying a room marked Closet with the door propped open, he ducked inside.

It was dark inside, and Zane shrank back into the shadows of the corner, hoping Lieutenant Mike would just walk on by. But he didn't. No one did. The hall sounded as silent and deserted as this closet. He crept forward, edging toward the door carefully.

Then it slammed shut.

There was darkness. Then startling bright light as Zane stared up into a dark, angry-looking face.

Every muscle in Brooks's body tensed as a knock sounded at his door. He gripped the captain's gun in his right hand under the covers. "Come in."

Mike stuck his head around the edge. "How are you?"

Blowing out a sigh of relief, Brooks nodded.

Chuckling irreverently, the pudgy detective crossed the room. "What do you think, Brooks, that Dante would knock? I don't think he has those kind of manners."

"I hear you." A glance at his watch told Brooks it was after four. "Anything going on?"

"This place is like a tomb." Mike shivered. "Jeez, I hate hospitals."

"Me, too."

"You think they'll let you out tomorrow?"

"I hope so."

"And then are you going to make up with Holly?"

Brooks merely grunted. His friends and family had noticed Holly's not being here. He had told them the truth—that he had ended it. And he had steadfastly refused to discuss it with anyone. He wasn't about to start now.

Another knock sounded at the door before Mike could push for more information. The detective rolled his eyes. "It's probably Donna. Last time I saw her, she was fighting sleep hard."

"Come on in," Brooks called.

A hospital guard whom Brooks had already seen twice tonight stepped inside. "I hate to bother you," he said, "but I was wondering if you'd seen Holly MacPherson's little boy."

"Zane?" Brooks and Mike said together.

The guard nodded. "No one's seen him since about eight last night, when he supposedly went to bed. Miss MacPherson's grandmother called and said she thought he might have come here to see you. I decided to come up and check."

"I haven't seen him," Brooks said, frowning in concern.

"And I've been round and round this hospital all night," Mike added.

"Well, I'll keep looking," the guard said, backing toward the door.

"I'll help you." Mike started to follow the man out.

But Brooks called him back, struck by a sudden terrible thought. "If Zane is really missing and Dante's out there..."

Mike sucked in his breath, a horrified look on his face. "Jesus, Brooks, no." Jerking the radio out of his belt, he called for all units to start looking immediately for Zane. Wheeling around, he said, "Don't worry, Brooks. I'm going to find him."

But after Mike left, Brooks couldn't sit and wait. He pulled himself out of bed. His head felt four sizes too big, and he was wobbly, but he could walk. The hard part was shrugging into his robe with his left shoulder so stiff and painful. But he didn't think anyone would let him go wandering through the halls in just the boxer shorts he was wearing, especially since he needed to take his gun with him.

The hall outside was darkened and deserted. He moved away from the nurses' station, certain they'd try to stop him. He ducked down one hall and up another, into stairwells and down to the next floor. Brooks wasn't sure how long he searched. Every corner looked the same. There were so many turns, so many rooms where someone could hide, where someone could have a little boy.

He didn't pass any guards. Where the hell were they? With all these halls and all these rooms, they needed a hundred guards to search for one little boy. Why in God's name weren't there hundreds already here, looking for that boy?

What would he do if Dante hurt Zane? The question put speed to Brooks's steps as he clambered down the stairs again. He would never forgive himself. Damn it, why hadn't he thought about putting a guard back at Holly's when Dixon brought in that note tonight? Granted, all he'd been trying to do was forget Holly. He had thrown her away. Thrown away her love. Even though he loved her...

As he careened around a corner on the first floor, pain shot through Brooks's head. He had to grab hold of the railing along the wall and stand there for a minute to get his breath.

He loved Holly. In the panic of this moment, Brooks let himself admit that. He loved her. He finally knew what that emotion was. He loved her and

Zane. And he had probably blown it, blown the only chance at happiness a man like him was likely to get. And if Dante got Zane, if he hurt the boy because of Brooks...

Oh, God, he would never forgive himself.

Emotions thundered through Brooks's brain as he gripped the handrail and tried to stand. His shoulder felt wet, as if it might be bleeding. And his legs felt heavy as he turned.

But when he did... there was Zane.

Running down the hall, calling his name, here came Zane. Holly's boy. *His boy.*

"Sweet Jesus!" Bad shoulder forgotten, Brooks knelt and caught the boy up in his arms. Like that day at Holly's house when the boy had run out to meet them, all Brooks could do was hold him and say his name again and again. But unlike that day, this time Brooks let his tears flow.

Crying like a baby, he clutched his boy to his heart.

"Brooks, Brooks," Zane said, anxiously pushing away. "You're bleedin'. Brooks, are you all right?"

Brooks finally found his voice. "Yeah, son, I am. Now that I know you're okay, I'm just fine. But where were you? What happened?"

"I came looking for you," Zane explained. "And I was trying not to get caught and Mrs. Coulter found me hiding in a closet."

With a muffled cry of thanksgiving, Brooks pulled the boy back into his arms. He wondered if he'd ever get enough of hugging him. Raising his eyes to heaven, he thanked God for this boy.

And that's when he saw Holly.

She stood just a few feet away, leaning against the wall. Her hand covered her mouth, and tears streamed from her dark, dark eyes. Eyes filled with tenderness.

Setting Zane aside, Brooks put his hand to the rail and struggled to pull himself up. Holly was immediately at his side. Dimly, Brooks was aware of Mike appearing from somewhere and taking hold of Zane.

But Brooks could only look at Holly. Burning with shame for all he had said to her yesterday, he couldn't seem to utter a word.

"You liar," she murmured, helping him stand. "You dirty, rotten liar."

"I'm sorry."

"You didn't mean any of what you said to me."

"Not a word."

"You almost killed me."

He bowed his head, hands gripping the railing. "I'm sorry, Holly. I'll spend the rest of my days being sorry for that. Please forgive me."

"You're the reason Zane ran away tonight."

"I know. When I heard..." He swallowed hard. "Dante says he's after me again."

She nodded. "Mike told me when I got to the hospital. Everyone was going crazy looking for you by then."

Head spinning, Brooks let out a long sigh of relief. "What about Dante?"

"You can ask Mike about him later. Let's get you to your room now."

"No, I want to make sure that creep can't touch you or Zane." Even as he said the words, Brooks felt his body begin to sag.

Holly took firmer hold of his arm. "Forget about Dante, will you? Your shoulder is bleeding and you're white as a sheet. What were you thinking—taking off through the hospital?"

"I had to find Zane." Closing his eyes, Brooks felt darkness pulling at him.

"I think you love him a little."

"A lot. Almost as much as I love you."

Brooks just managed to open his eyes to see the joy that spread across Holly's face before he blacked out.

Sunshine was beaming in through the blinds when Brooks next opened his eyes. From the angle of the light, he figured it was well into the afternoon. But that wasn't the reason for the warmth along the right side of his body. That came from Holly. She had crawled into his hospital bed beside him. And she was watching him. Her gaze brought him wide awake.

"Do you always come awake like that?" she teased.

"Like what?"

"Like a big old bear coming out of hibernation."

"I don't know. Maybe you can take notes for the rest of our lives and tell me."

"The rest of our lives." Her smile rivaled the sunshine. "So you meant it last night?"

"What?"

"You do love me?"

"Absolutely."

"I thought maybe you were just weak from loss of blood."

"No way." Cupping a hand around the back of her neck, he pulled her face down to meet his and pressed a soft, gentle kiss on her lips. "I meant everything I said last night, Holly. I'm so sorry for the way I hurt you. I was trying to push you away. I've just watched so many cops and their families suffer...." Breaking off, he studied her for a moment. "And I know you never wanted to be married to a cop."

She touched his cheek. "I want to marry *you*. And as my wise Nana has always told me, what people do is part of who they are. And I love every part of you, Brooks Casey."

Pushing a hand through Holly's thick, shining hair, he whispered, "As soon as this mess with Dante is over—"

"But it is," Holly said.

Brooks pulled away. "How?"

She sat up, her brown eyes very solemn. "He's dead."

"Dead." It took a minute for the knowledge to sink in. "But how?" he demanded, then grunted in pain as he lifted his shoulders off the bed. "What in the hell happened?"

Instead of answering the questions he kept shooting at her, Holly slid off the bed and fussed over him, rearranging the pillows under his head and injured shoulder and raising the bed so that he was most comfortable. Before she was through, there was a tap on the door and in walked Mike and Donna.

"What happened?" Brooks barked at them.

The two detectives traded pained looks.

"Jeez, what a rude character," Mike muttered. "You'd think he'd at least say hello."

Donna held up a white sack. "And here I brought him some doughnuts. His favorite kind—chocolate glazed. Maybe I'll keep 'em—"

"Okay, okay," Brooks interrupted. "I'm sorry. Hello to you both. Now what happened to Dante?"

Mike shot Holly a glance. "Have you told him anything?"

"Just that Dante's dead," she replied.

"They caught him at the airport," Donna said, dropping the sack of doughnuts at Brooks's side.

He looked at her in surprise. "Why there? I thought he was coming after me."

Shaking his head, Mike muttered, "That coward. He was heading back to the Caribbean."

Brooks let out a long, slow breath. "So coming after me was just a smoke screen." He was trying not to think of the nightmare he'd lived through last night when he thought Dante could be in this hospital with Zane as his hostage. "But how'd he end up dead?"

"Markowitz," Donna supplied.

Stunned, Brooks stared at the three somber faces around his bed. From their sorrowful expressions you'd think that Markowitz was...that he might be... Thoughts of what might have happened to his young partner sent Brooks scrambling out from under the covers.

Holly caught one arm and Mike grabbed the other as Brooks swung his feet out of bed. Together, they kept him from getting up.

"Whoa, buddy," the portly detective cautioned. "Don't go getting all worked up. Sit back."

"But Markowitz—"

"Is fine," Donna quickly reassured him. "He decided to check out the airport where Dante's dimwitted nephew used to keep a small plane. He was over there while the rest of us were scrambling around here."

"And his hunch paid off. Dante showed up." Sighing in relief, Brooks took hold of Holly's hand and held it tight.

"The old weasel put up a fight," Mike said. "In the end, Markowitz had no choice but to take Dante and one of his goons down."

"And Markowitz is okay?" Brooks asked.

"As okay as you can be after something like that," Donna murmured.

Brooks nodded, knowing exactly what Markowitz was going through. The young detective would need a friend who had faced the same situation. Brooks planned to be there for him.

Holly squeezed his fingers lightly with her own. "Mike had just gotten word about this when Mrs. Coulter found Zane hiding in a closet."

"And you turned up missing," Mike put in, scowling. "Of all the damn fool—"

"I had to find Zane," Brooks said, looking at Holly. "I had to find my boy."

Holly had read about moments when the world just slipped away. And certainly a look from Brooks had sent her spinning many times before. But never like this. All that existed was her and him and the love shining from his eyes.

Dimly, she heard Donna shooing Mike out of the room. Vaguely, she recognized Nana Flora's laughter and Zane's excited young voice out in the hall. Faintly, she realized that the door didn't latch behind Donna and Mike's retreat. But she didn't care. There would be plenty of time for celebrating with her son. Now, she just wanted to savor Brooks and this single, perfect moment.

"I love you," she whispered.

He pulled her onto the bed. "The feeling's mutual."

"And I love that you love Zane, too."

"So you think you and me and him might make it?"

As she looked into his eyes, the eyes of the man she loved, Holly was certain of success. "Let's get married day after tomorrow," she suggested. "At midnight."

"Why?"

"Well, I hear there's gonna be an Elvis moon."

Laughing, Brooks caught her mouth beneath his again.

In the hospital hall, Zane flashed his aluminum-foil-covered sword. If he closed his eyes, he could almost imagine trumpets blaring, flags waving, crowds cheering. And all for him. He could see himself, victorious, astride a big horse, riding across a drawbridge into a stone castle.

Because, judging from all the kissing in the next room, his quest was complete.

*   *   *   *   *

Get ready to be swept away
by Silhouette's

Abduction &
SEDUCTION

These passion-filled stories explore both the
dangerous desires of men and the seductive
powers of women. Written by three of our most
celebrated authors, they are sure to capture
your hearts.

Diana Palmer
One of the world's top romance authors and
a mesmerising storyteller.

Joan Johnston
Enthrals us with red-hot passion.

Rebecca Brandewyne
New York Times bestselling author makes
a scintillating contemporary debut.

Available in May   *Price £4.99*

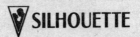 SILHOUETTE

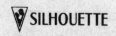
COMING NEXT MONTH

**Our next six Celebration 1,000 titles!
Join us as we celebrate our first 1,000 books and
the everlasting magic of romance!**

THE PRIDE OF JARED MACKADE
Nora Roberts

*1000th Book and the second in Nora Roberts' latest
mini-series—The MacKade Brothers*

Jared MacKade was used to getting his way—especially with
women. But he was getting nowhere with gorgeous Savannah
Morningstar. The lady was wreaking havoc with his pride,
and when a MacKade's pride got stepped on, there was bound
to be hell to pay…

DADDY'S GIRL
Barbara Bretton

Devoting his life to the care of his eight month old niece
meant Hunter Phillips was suddenly a one-woman man…until
he met Jeannie Ross. Jeannie knew all about babies, but did
she have any idea of the effect she was having on Hunter?

A PERFECT MARRIAGE
Laurey Bright

Celine and Max Archer appeared to have the perfect marriage,
and only they knew it was just a dry-eyed deal. Then Max
broke the bargain—by wanting more. When Celine realized
how much she loved her husband, was it too late to get him
back?

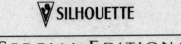

COMING NEXT MONTH

ELEANORA'S GHOST
Suzanne Carey

Pretty Elly Raftree had never met anyone who affected her quite the way Daniel Brant did. She knew a man as magnetic as Daniel would have women falling at his feet wherever he went, so why did he appear so interested in her?

HERE TO STAY
Kate Freiman

A patch of black ice and Miles Kent's vintage car—and his memory—were history. All the bitter amnesiac had was a gentle woman to save him. Tender Sasha Reiss took him into her home, into her heart…and into her bed…

MORGAN'S RESCUE
Lindsay McKenna

Morgan's Mercenaries

There was no way Culver Lachlan would team up with beautiful Pilar Martinez for a new mission. Seeing her again brought back bitter memories of how she'd abandoned their love, yet reminded him of the torrid passion they'd once shared…

THE MEN OF MIDNIGHT

Three men born at the stroke of twelve and destined for love beyond their wildest dreams.

Award-winning author Emilie Richards launches her new mini-series, **The Men of Midnight**, in May 1996 with *Duncan's Lady*.

Single father Duncan Sinclair believed in hard facts and cold reality, not mist and magic. But Mara MacTavish challenged his masculinity and his hard-line beliefs. Her warmth and charm captivated both Duncan and his young daughter.

The Men of Midnight traces the friendship between Duncan, Iain and Andrew. Don't miss *Iain Ross's Woman* in June and *MacDougall's Darling* concluding the trilogy in July.

Return this coupon and we'll send you 4 Silhouette Special Editions and a mystery gift absolutely FREE! We'll even pay the postage and packing for you.

We're making you this offer to introduce you to the benefits of Reader Service: FREE home delivery of brand-new Silhouette romances, at least a month before they are available in the shops, FREE gifts and a monthly Newsletter packed with information.

Accepting these FREE books and gift places you under no obligation to buy, you may cancel at any time, even after receiving just your free shipment. Simply complete the coupon below and send it to:

SILHOUETTE READER SERVICE, FREEPOST, CROYDON, CR9 3WZ.

No stamp needed

Yes, please send me 4 free Silhouette Special Editions and a mystery gift. I understand that unless you hear from me, I will receive 6 superb new titles every month for just £2.30* each postage and packing free. I am under no obligation to purchase any books and I may cancel or suspend my subscription at any time, but the free books and gifts will be mine to keep in any case. (I am over 18 years of age)

1EP6SE

Ms/Mrs/Miss/Mr _____

Address _____

_____

_____ Postcode _____

COMING NEXT MONTH FROM
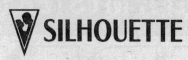 SILHOUETTE

Intrigue
Danger, deception and desire

DROP-DEAD GORGEOUS Patricia Rosemoor
DARK KNIGHT Sheryl Lynn
UNLAWFULLY WEDDED Kelsey Roberts
LYING EYES Erika Rand

Desire
Provocative, sensual love stories for the woman of today

FATHER IN THE MAKING Marie Ferrarella
CALHOUN Diana Palmer
COWBOYS DON'T STAY Anne McAllister
ESCAPADES Cathie Linz
TEXAS PRIDE Barbara McCauley
STARTING OVER Andrea Edwards

Sensation
A thrilling mix of passion, adventure and drama

AN IRRESISTIBLE MAN Kylie Brant
A FATHER'S CLAIM Kim Cates
DUNCAN'S LADY Emilie Richards
WHO'S THE BOSS? Linda Turner